LOVE IN THE AGE OF REPTILES

by
Wayne Kyle Spitzer

 Published by Hobb's End Books, a division of ACME Sprockets & Visions. Please direct all inquiries to: HobbsEndBooks@yahoo.com

The Flashback/Dinosaur
Apocalypse Cycle

Flashback
(re-printed in *Dinosaur Apocalypse*)

Flashback Dawn
(re-printed in *Dinosaur Apocalypse*)

Tales from the Flashback
(re-printed as *Dinosaur Rampage*)

Flashback Twilight
(serialized as *A Dinosaur is a Man's Best Friend;*
re-printed as *The Complete Ank & Williams,*
Dinosaur War, Paladins)

A Reign of Thunder
(serialized as *Heat Wave,* collected in
The Lost Country [book], Escape from Seattle)

A Survivor's Guide to the
Dinosaur Apocalypse
(collected as *Dinosaur Carnage,* and in
The Lost Country [book] and *Escape from Seattle*)

The Lost Country: The Series

The Big Empty

Photographers call it the golden hour, that period of time right before sunset when the sky glows orange and the shadows lose their edges, and the world becomes, for the space of about 20 minutes, something elevated and painterly—ephemeral, even sublime. Add to that the ocean breaking over the rocks and the black and white 19th century lighthouse, and, well, you have some idea of how seeing Granite Point that first time affected us (when we were taking it all in by Jeep, whose top we'd removed in spite of the pterodactyls swarming the beach). So, too, were there the strange lights in the sky, which peered down, relentlessly, disapprovingly, as though we had no right to even celebrate (by going on what Amelia had called our "post-apocalyptic honeymoon"), nor to end our crushing isolation.

Beyond that, though, beyond the fact that it was the golden hour and the waves were crashing and that one side of the lighthouse gleamed like polished brass (or that we were still euphoric over having encountered each other less than 24 hours before), beyond all that was our shared epiphany; which was that the lantern, far from being illuminated from without, was, now that we'd had a chance to observe it up close, shining from within. That it had somehow been kept on—either by electricity or gas or the burning of oil or kerosene—and that it would have had to have been carefully maintained. Which meant that someone, somehow, someone just like us, perhaps, had managed to survive.

"It's beautiful," said Amelia—and swallowed, batting away the tears. "My God, Francis. Look at it. I never thought—"

"That you'd see a light again, I know." I peered at the house attached to the tower's base and the old truck parked in its drive—which looked to be in surprisingly good shape. "Nor did I." I looked at her sidelong and gave her a little wink. "But then, I didn't expect *you,* either."

She didn't notice, only continued staring at the lantern house, as if she were in a daze. "It shifts ... the light. First white, then blue, then purple. And then a color—sort of like bottle green, only iridescent. Like a mallard's neck. And yet shot through with ..."

She looked at me as if for help.

"Beats me," I said. "I'm color blind. Red-green color deficiency. Either way, I suggest we make contact—if we're going to. It'll be too dangerous after dark."

She seemed to come out of it, whatever *it* was. “Is that a good idea? I mean, with just our knives?”

“No,” I said, studying the darkened house. “But—whoever they are—they’re using *something* for power.” I lifted my gaze to the rotating lamp. “Enough to turn and illuminate that thing. And I’d like to know what it is.” I looked at her across the cab, which was bathed in golden light. “Wouldn’t you?”

And we just stared at each other: there by the lighthouse at Granite Point on the Oregon coast, after the time-storm—the Flashback, as someone had called it at the beginning—the dinosaur apocalypse. After everyone had vanished and the entire world had become a landscape of cycads and ruins, a place inhabited by winds and the souls of winds, a lost country.

“Jesus. Just—Jesus,” said Amelia, staring at the decomposing body. “How long do you think it’s been here?”

I examined it where it was sprawled on the back porch, facing the ocean, its skin blackened and clinging to the bones—like it had been vacuum sealed—its wispy hair fluttering. "Hard to say. Few weeks. Maybe a month.” I batted away the flies. “Long enough for the organs to liquify.”

"How–how do you know?"

I studied the holes in its head, a smaller one which was about the size of a dime and a larger, more cavernous one–the exit wound. "Because, otherwise, there'd be brains all over." I stepped over it and picked up the gun, checked its chamber. "There's still bullets in it."

She stared at me tentatively as I closed the chamber and gripped the weapon in both hands–neither of us saying anything. At last I nodded to the back door–the screen of which banged back and forth in the wind–and tried to brace myself. "You ready?"

She shook her head.

"Let's go," I said.

And then she was holding the screen as I inched forward and gripped the knob–turning it slowly, carefully, easing the door open. Stepping into a room which was dark as pitch; which reeked of cat piss and despair.

We worked well together, that much was clear; it was evidenced by how we swept and cleared the house so efficiently, Amelia opening the curtains (to let in more light) even as I scrambled to quick-check the rooms and closet spaces–finding a radio with batteries in it as well as some flashlights; not to mention a pantry full of food (mainly jars and jars of canned fish—salmon and snapper, according to the labels). Still, what I *didn't* find was any evidence of a non-electric power source for the lantern; something which seemed impossible—given the grid had failed shortly after the Flashback and the house itself was completely inert. Nor would this have gone unexamined—that is, if not for the discovery of the door; by which I mean the padlocked door to the tower itself, which we stumbled across at virtually the same instant—or so it seemed—having found it tucked away in a kind of antechamber in the furthermost section of the home.

"But, why the hell would he lock it?" I confess I was flummoxed.

Amelia frowned. "Why wouldn't he? He probably felt as though he were the only one that—I don't know, could be trusted with it. To maintain it. Especially after the Flashback." She fingered a small hook next to the door. "That's odd—don't you think?"

I stared at the hook. It was the only thing that *wasn't.*

"It's probably on that corpse; the key, I mean."

She looked up at me fetchingly, her brown eyes—she said they were green—flicking up and down my body, once, twice.

"Now wait just a damn minute,"

"Now you wouldn't promise me a lighthouse and then fail to deliver, would you?" She ran her hands over my shirt and up the sides of my neck, cupping my face in her palms, tilting her head. "I mean, we *are* on our honeymoon—aren't we? And who knows what a girl might do if escorted to the top of that beautiful beacon with the waves crashing all around her and the seabirds—"

"Pterodactyls," I corrected her. "They're pterodactyls. And they'll peck your eyes out."

"Whatever," she rasped, and brushed my lips with her own. "What are you afraid of? That you'll catch the Ebola virus? Or maybe smallpox? The 1918 flu?"

"What I'm afraid of," I lowered her hands gently. "Is that we're going to lose the light and get stuck here. Like, all night." I looked at her sternly. "And I don't think you want that."

She picked at and adjusted my shirt collar, undeterred. "Why not? I mean, where else should we go? Back to Walmart? Back to those little settees in Home Furnishings, with their hard, hard little cushions—where you were such a gentleman, I might add, to just talk to me and assuage my doubts, and to not try so much as a—"

There was a sound, a kind of warbling yowl, a drawn-out, caterwauling, doleful cry, which rose up from the nearby trees and reverberated along the shoreline—where it was promptly answered by another, and yet another.

Neither of us moved.

At last I said: "That was a pit raptor."

Nobody said anything as the waves crashed against the rocks and the pterodactyls squawked.

"Out on the point? That's impossible."

"No, it's not. They're night hunters. They're just beginning their workday."

"But—"

"Shhh. Listen."

The sound came again—briefer, this time, more succinct, as though the animal was moving.

I looked around the room—my heart pounding, but there were no windows, no way to tell what was going on outside. "We've got to go. Like, now. Before—"

"But, don't you see? That's what I was trying to tell you. *We took the top down."*

I froze, feeling as though the walls were closing in—like I might actually pass out. But then—then it just passed, I can't really explain it, and I was myself again (the "cool cucumber," as Amelia had described me), and what's more, I'd accepted it. Accepted that I had led us blunderingly into a bad situation because I had hoped, in some dim quarter of my mind—and this despite it being the end of the world itself—to make time with her.

Amelia. The girl I'd met in a ruined Walmart in Coos Bay while scrounging for a pair of shoes—again, while the sun was going down—as well as something to eat. I guess one didn't know whether to laugh or to cry. Either way, one thing had become clear. And that was that, for this night, anyway—we weren't going anywhere.

Now, you might ask: Didn't I find it odd that she'd be so adamant on sleeping separately—in spite of the cold and her earlier flirtatiousness—that we had to drag a bed into the antechamber? And my answer is: No. Not really. Rather, I just took it to mean she was establishing a boundary, and that the apocalypse itself couldn't turn her into something she wasn't—which, frankly, I respected. Besides, any man who knows anything knows the coin paid going in is the same earned staying out, which is to say Time, however scrambled it had become, was on my side, and I knew it.

More than any of that, though, was that I wanted to try out the radio, which I did, drinking scotch from the caretaker's stash and looking out the window—which framed the breakers and gathered pterodactyls like a picture—wrapped in one of the keeper's thick, filthy blankets. At which I was delighted to discover that the batteries were good and that it in fact worked– and so began scrubbing the dial; hoping, against hope, to catch something, anything (an emergency broadcast signal, a test tone, *anything*) but finding only static; until, suddenly, even as I was about to give up, there were a flurry of sounds—sounds such as I hadn't heard since before the Flashback—which, taken together, constituted a thing I'd thought no longer possible, a thing as extinct as the terrible lizards themselves, which I turned down immediately in order to keep all to myself, and soaked up as though fresh from the desert—marinating in it, breathing it all in, drowning.

Woah, Georgia ... Geoorrgia ... No peace, no peace I find. Just an old, sweet song, keeps Georgia, on my miiind ....

I think I must have sunk to the floor, sunk to it in a veritable puddle, spilling the bottle of scotch which clinked and sloshed, forgetting about the cold and the lantern and the pit raptors—which may or may not have still been out there—forgetting the lost country and its hopelessness.

I said just an old, sweet song, keeps Georgia ... on my miiind ...

Until it was over, and the instruments and back-up singers had all faded to nothing, and a voice came on—a new voice, a speaking voice; a *woman's* voice—and said, mellifluously, "And that was the immortal Ray Charles, with "Georgia on my Mind."

And this—this is Radio Free Montana—with Bella Ray, broadcasting from Barley Hot Springs in what some used to call the Great White North—which was not intended as a compliment." She laughed. "So just trust in God and keep your powder dry; and stay with us here wherever you may be—whether that's a cold water flat in Devil's Lake, North Dakota, or a high-rise hotel in Miami-Dade—wherever you are out there in the Big Empty, we here at KAAR-RFM will try to have your back. And now it's back to the music and Patsy Cline, with "Walking After Midnight." Take it away, Patsy!"

I was up and moving down the hall almost before I'd realized it, double-timing it for Amelia's room, using one of the flashlights I'd found to see the way, knocking on her door (which seemed thick as a vault now that I thought about it and just sort of absorbed the sound, like solid rock).

Jesus, I remember thinking. I'd searched for a mere signal and found a whole community! It was like we'd gotten rescued from *Gilligan's Island;* escaped from the *Land of the Lost.* Like we'd come home from Oz itself. And I simply couldn't wait to tell her— although how the music hadn't awakened her was completely beyond me. I mean, surely—

But she didn't answer the door, which seemed impossible, not even when I pounded on it with my fists, which literally shook off paint peelings.

"Amelia!" I shouted. "Amelia!" I pounded again and again. "Wake up, Amelia!"

Until at last I thought, *Fuck this,* and tried the knob—only to find it locked. At which I resolved to kick it in (fat chance), or find an ax (she could be dying in there!), and was backing away from it to try just that, when it occurred to me I was acting like a psychopath and a fool.

The fact was, she was a heavy sleeper, I'd seen it myself the previous night. And she was in the habit of wrapping the pillow about her head, which would have further blunted any sound. And that door—Jesus Christ.

I wandered back into the living room and turned off the radio, to conserve the batteries. It would just have to wait until morning, like digging the key out of the corpse's pocket. The fact was—everything was going to be all right. And with that I found another bottle of liquor—Jeppson's Malört, whatever the fuck that was—and settled in on the couch; after which the grandfather clock struck 8 and what looked a plesiosaur, only huge, like a small whale, leapt from the ocean—to snatch one of the pterodactyls from the orange-painted rocks.

"What, you've never wondered if you dreamt something or actually experienced it? Happens to me. And you said it yourself: you were shit-canned off that—what was it?"

"Jeppson's Malört," I said—still tasting it in my mouth, smelling it on my sweat. Still feeling as though it had been poured over my brain like bile. "Look, it wasn't a dream, okay?"

I stopped walking and stared at her—to emphasize my point—as seabirds swirled (there were no pterodactyls today) and the waves crashed. "Look, I know it's hard to believe, but I'm telling you: Someone is on the air." I gripped her shoulders—harder than I'd intended. "Radio Free Montana—that's what they call themselves. Broadcasting out of a place called Barley Hot Springs. Jesus, Amelia. Don't you see what that means?"

She placed her hands on her hips. "Have you listened to yourself?" She briefly put her face in her palm. "How would a signal even get from there to here, without—I don't know, a relay of some kind. What you're saying is *crazy,* Francis—can't you see that?" She shook her head as if in pity. "I mean, can't you?"

"I'm not crazy," I said, and took my hands off her. "I heard what I heard. And we've got to go there—like, now, today. While the sun is shining. I swear, I'll—" I looked back at the lighthouse and the old truck parked near our Jeep. "I'll go alone if I have to."

She picked up a couple pieces of driftwood, first one, then the other, looking exasperated. "Then why aren't they broadcasting anymore? Riddle me that, Francis. And why aren't you gathering wood for the fire? For that matter; why aren't you burying our friend?"

"There's maggots," I said–and started walking, finding it strange she hadn't mentioned the key. "I'm working up to it. And to hell with the fire. You're just trying to change the subject."

"Oh, I see. Well–isn't that what we came out here for? To gather wood?" She hurried to catch up with me. "Or would you prefer to freeze again tonight? You know: and to pickle yourself in Jeppson's Merlot, like–"

"Malört," I said, increasing my pace. "Besides, I don't plan on being here. And neither should you."

She stopped abruptly and called after me, "Then where are you going?"

I took a few more steps and then paused–but didn't turn around. "I was just walking–if you want to know the truth. Figured it would do us some good. But now–now I want to look at *that.*" And I pointed.

At the beach grasses which had been singed and lain down nearly flat–as if a burning helicopter had set down directly in their midst—and the saltbushes twisted into an insidious vortex. At the mounds and mounds of sand and other sediment which had been dredged up and redeposited—in an approximate circle—by some presently unseen force (a bulldozer, perhaps); or an object from space having made sudden, violent impact.

“What do you suppose it was?” asked Amelia, poking the ashy dirt with one of her sticks, stirring it around.

“I wouldn’t do that,” I warned. “Could be unexploded ordinance—you never know.”

She gasped and moved back—although not very far—as I studied the point of impact, noting how angular it was, how geometrical (as if a giant arrowhead had been stabbed into the earth); all of which left me to wonder—had the object somehow been removed? Or was it still down there?

I scanned the area, looking for debris. “There’s no wreckage—which is odd. So I doubt it was a satellite. No; I’m afraid there’s only two possibilities, really. Bomb or meteorite. And I doubt very much it was a bomb.”

“Or *is?*”

“Or is.”

She didn't say anything, only continued staring into the dirt.

At last I said, "What is it?"

"Nothing ... it ... it's nothing." She seemed dazed, confused. "It's just that ... it all seems so strange now. I mean—that we ever had use for such things. For bombs. That we could spend so much time and effort and money ... just to kill each other."

She looked out at the ocean and the billowing clouds, the whirling seabirds, the distant pterodactyls. "That we could make such ugliness and pain—such sheer terror—and in such a beautiful world. I mean, *look* at it, Francis. Can you honestly say that it's not better off without us? Or that, even if there are other people, we're not better off without them?"

I must have looked confused. "What the hell are you talking about?"

She turned to face me; her dark eyes close to mine. "Give me one reason, Francis. Give me one reason why we shouldn't just stay here, forever—you and I, alone. Give me one reason why we shouldn't restore the lighthouse and defend it and kill anyone who comes close; why we shouldn't go so far as to kill them first—just kill them where they sleep—and stop the threat before it even begins. Tell me now why they're worth saving, and why we shouldn't finish what *they* started," She nodded briskly at the sky, "What they instigated with the Flashback but failed to complete. What can be completed still–"

And I kissed her, suddenly, completely–I'm still not sure why, maybe because I thought she was breaking down and that doing so would be the only way to snap her out of it, to shock her back to her senses. All I know is that she responded almost immediately and we stayed like that for some time, kissing not as children lost in a storm–which is how it had felt that first night when she'd pecked me on the lips before retreating to her own settee–but as something akin to red hot lovers: thirstily, intensely, primally (but not base), the Bogie and Bacall of the apocalypse.

After which I said, "Maybe you shouldn't be alone tonight."

And she said: "Not yet." And then kissed me again.

Until the moment (and the day) had passed and we'd agreed to stay one more night, and she'd retired by 8 pm to the antechamber while I drank vodka on the couch, shortly after which a plesiosaur breached the froth like a glistening killer whale–and snatched a pterodactyl from the orange-painted rocks.

I'm not going to lie; I hadn't really expected to find it—the key—regardless of what I'd expressed previously; so, imagine my surprise when I searched the corpse's stained pockets—managing, somehow, to keep a tenuous grasp on my breakfast—and touched a crenulated edge.

Bingo, I remember thinking, not lastly because it seemed to absolve Amelia—whom I'd come to suspect had taken it and not told me—but also because it would allow me to test something; something I'd been thinking about a lot since discovering the strange crater. One of *many* things I'd been thinking about.

I peered up at the lantern as the rain fell and the clouds drifted, as the melancholy of the day hung over everything like a shroud. *Tell me now why humanity is worth saving, and why we shouldn't finish what They started. What They instigated with the Flashback but failed to complete. What can be completed still.*

The words sat on my stomach like poached eggs. Absolved her? Perhaps. But not explained anything.

I gazed along the beach: at the desolate breakers and the gray tide rolling in, at the vortex of saltbushes about a half mile away—flies buzzing my face as I did so. I wasn't ready for this shit. For burying the lighthouse keeper. Then I started walking (wondering, as I went, what the weather was like in Montana, and if they had children there—and if so, were they happy and well-provided for?) ... until at last I came to the crater; where I quickly noticed something which should have been obvious the day before (but somehow hadn't been), and that was that it was incredibly close to the road itself—and that, indeed, they were separated only by a sandy embankment. An embankment, I soon realized, which still had drag marks in it—as though someone had unearthed whatever had fallen and pulled it up to the road.

I looked back the way I'd come—the rain pelting my jacket, the wind buffeted my hair.

As though someone had loaded it onto a truck; and then driven it—not bothering to pass "Go" or to collect $200—back to the lighthouse at Granite Point.

"Amelia?" I knocked on her door gently but firmly. "The Jeep's all ready to go. Also, I—I buried the keeper. I mean it's pretty shallow, but ... it'll have to do."

I waited a moment to see if she'd answer. When she didn't, I added: "And there's something else. Something I want to show you."

Still no answer. Only the breathing of the ocean, the ticking of the grandfather clock. I knocked again.

"Amelia? *Hey.* You there?"

That's when I knew. That's when I knew she'd had the key all along—had it since before I'd even discovered the antechamber; since she'd found it on the hook next to the lighthouse door—and that she must have planted it on the keeper only recently, possibly even the previous night.

And then I was turning the knob and the door was opening—just swinging in as easy as could be—and my shadow had fallen across her bed which was piled with blankets and clothes; after which, sweating and trembling, I looked at the lighthouse door—and saw that it was lazed open.

And began to move toward it.

I saw it even before I saw her—a spearpoint-shaped thing, an impossible thing, a thing blacker than black yet giving off light—which levitated straight as an arrow at the center of the Fresnel and somehow caused it to turn, to warp, to change its shape and then back again, to be at once physical yet abstract. Nor was it the size of even the largest lightbulbs but rather tall as a man, with no surface features whatsoever—like one of those cars which has been painted Vantablack and so absorbs all incidental light—a thing as perfect as it was paradoxical, and which had no color of its own yet somehow radiated multitudes.

A thing beyond which—out on the catwalk—stood Amelia: barefoot but wrapped in the keeper's bathrobe; facing away from the black light and myself; facing the sea which rose up and crashed on the rocks.

I circled around toward her but paused, gripping the doorframe. "H-Hello? Amelia? What—what are you doing out there? Are you okay?"

She didn't respond, only continued facing the sea (and the seabirds, which swirled like moths), her hair whipping and lashing—pulsing and glowing—appearing as though it were on fire as I crept onto the catwalk and approached her with caution. As she dropped the robe from her body—revealing herself to be completely nude—and I reached for her shoulder, slowly turning her around.

At which she said, "Careful, it'll eat your eyes," and looked up at me with eyes that had become black glass—like black, interstellar voids—and yet, *not,* because they were also full of light; full of pulsars and quasars and nebulae and supernovae; of blue giants and red dwarfs and white fountains and stellar flares—and colors which could not be defined much less comprehended—hues I should not have been able to see but could!

All of which was the moment I looked at the clouds and understood—and knew at once what the queer object was—for it was nothing less than one of the strange lights in the sky; nothing less than one of the architects of the Flashback itself—one that had fallen to Earth like a shooting star and been recovered by the lighthouse keeper after the Collapse (and which he had then placed inside his Fresnel). One that had gotten into Amelia and was in her even now, whispering to her, I realized—even as I backed into the lantern house and she quickly followed—guiding her. Compelling her toward some end I hadn't the ability to imagine.

"You see it—I can tell you do," she said, having followed my gaze; having focused on the lights in the clouds, on *them*—whose colors were the same as those in her eyes. "You see it and yet do not fully understand it." She looked at me and tilted her head; began touching my lips, tracing them as though they were art. "Let it in, Francis. Let it in as I will let you in—here, now, in every way."

She lowered to her knees—smoothly, silkily—sliding her hands along my body, unfastening my pants. "They have work for us." She pushed up my shirt and began kissing my stomach. "Do it with me, Francis. Do the work. You said it yourself—they're in Montana. Take me there."

And then she was gripping me and taking me into her mouth, moving her lips up and down, as I put her head in my hands and looked at the thing, the anomaly, the perfect, black arrowhead which somehow emanated light, and which showed me things even as I looked at it—dreadful things, horrible things—images in which people were being murdered by their own trust and generosity; visions in which I saw an entire community lain to waste. Until I could take it no more—for it was the future I saw—and tore myself away: yanking up my trousers and hurrying for the hatch, clambering down the spiral staircase which pulsed and flashed with light, bursting into the antechamber and down the hall into the living room.

Where I snatched up a bottle of whisky and began drinking it raw and undiluted. Where I crumbled to the floor and moaned, wondering what to think or do.

They call it the golden hour, that period of time right before sunset when the sky glows orange and the shadows lose their edges, and the world becomes, for the space of about 20 minutes, something elevated and painterly—ephemeral, even sublime. That's how the world felt as I sat on the rocks and watched the waves crash and spume—

sublime. A thing of such grandeur and beauty that we couldn't help but to stand in awe. And yet, at the same time, weren't we part and parcel? Weren't we built of the same materials—the same *substantia primae*—and woven into its fabric like threads? And—that being the case—weren't we special too?

"You know it's funny," said Amelia, her voice sounding distant, muted, as though it were coming from a thousand miles away, "but somehow I knew you'd be here."

I looked up as she sat next to me—having put on a jacket like myself—and looked out at the sea, which crashed and breathed. "You always were more thoughtful than you let on," she said. She leaned into me with surprising intimacy. "More dutiful, more decent. It was the first thing I noticed about you."

I didn't say anything, only gazed out at the water and the swirling pterodactyls—one of which glided in for a landing.

At last she said: "It doesn't have to be this way, you know. We could pretend we never came here ... that nothing ever happened—even go our separate ways, if that's what you want."

I looked at my shoes—the ones I'd found at Walmart—and tried to smile. "You'd just come back. Back here, I mean. It—I think it's a part of you now. Part of your makeup."

Neither of us said anything as the birds squawked and wheeled and the sun sank toward the sea.

"Maybe. But does it matter? You'd be long gone. And who knows, maybe I can learn something from them. Something that ..." She trailed off; her face suddenly ashen.

"I'm sorry," I said, and gripped the gun. "But I—I can't let you do it. And I think we both know why."

She looked at me somewhat blankly before getting up slowly and walking to the edge of the breaker. "And so you're just going to casually blow me away, is that it? Just air me out, as they say?" She laughed, but when she turned to face me her eyes were full of compassion, not malice. "And you think you can really do that? Just whiff me out like a match?" She shook her head. "No you can't, Francis. I know you better than that—or I'd never come with you in the first place. Please. Put down the gun. You're not a murderer. Not even they could turn you into one. You know that."

I stood but kept the pistol trained on her, moving toward her slowly, closing the gap between us. "I'm not just going to stand by while you—while you kill the people of Barley. I—I'll never do that, Amelia. I'm sorry. And if that means ... If that means—"

"Shhh," she said. "Listen to yourself." She held her hand out between us. "Give me the gun, Francis. Please. You don't want to do this, I know. Give it to me."

I shook my head, trying to resist. There was something about her now; something about her eyes. Just a hint of strange color—a hint of *them*—which made them oddly hypnotic, oddly compelling. "I don't—I can't—"

And then she leapt forward—suddenly, violently— snatching the gun from my hand, shoving me from the rock—*hard*—turning it on me even as I got to my feet—my head bleeding from the fall.

"Well now—how the times change." She cocked the weapon decisively. "And to think it wanted me to kill you and I refused!"

I raised my hands even while avoiding her eyes. "Now, just—settle down, okay? Nobody's going to kill anybody. All right?" I took a step backward—focusing on the gun, on its 9mm barrel. "I mean, we're two for two—right? I spared you ... and now, hopefully, you'll spare me."

She didn't respond, only continued sighting me, her lower lip trembling.

At last she said, "It's crazy, isn't it? Pointing guns at each other—as though we've somehow been enemies and not friends." Her eyes began to well up markedly, profusely. *"I've never wanted to hurt you,*

Francis. But you have to understand, that–I'm no longer alone. That there's something else inside me now, and that it's vying–"

I stepped forward suddenly and she jerked the gun to track me.

"It's all right," I said. "It's all right. It's just that–"

And that's when it happened: that's when the silver and black plesiosaur breached the water like a mirage–its needle-teeth flashing and its dark neck glistening; its great flippers raked back like the wings of a plane–and snatched her from the rocks as though she were a doll. That's when the two of them seemed to hang briefly in the air–painted redden gold and burnt orange by the sun; rendered exquisite for a single fleeting instant–before crashing back to sea with a mighty smack and spray–and vanishing completely in its rough, roiling waters.

By the time I headed out the next day, the sun was at 12 o'clock and I'd fashioned two markers–one for the keeper and one for Amelia–both of which I'd planted atop breakers so they wouldn't be swept away. And then I'd made a sign–a sign for future travelers–which I'd hemmed and hawed over considerably before finally scrawling across it: GO TO BARLEY HOT SPRINGS IN MONTANA. STAY AWAY FROM THE LANTERN. Nor was it lost on me that the strange anomaly—who's very purpose had been to perpetuate the Flashback and thus usher men from the earth—would now be used to connect us; and to offer survivors hope. And I supposed that in the Big Empty, that was as good as it got.

And then I was off—having locked the tower door and disposed of its key—driving through Charleston and Barview and Coos Bay, following Tremont Avenue until it merged with Route 101, driving the Oregon Coast Highway all the way to Tillamook and beyond.

The Return

It was funny, that I should think of childhood for the second time that day (the first being when we'd descended the great tree next to the starship while still in our spacesuits, like kids playing astronaut). Still, there it was—just an image, really, a vignette—in this case a scene from a movie I'd seen at the East Fork Drive-in as a little boy (*Escape from the Planet of the Apes,* as I recalled, with Roddy McDowall and Kim Hunter), the one where the returned astronauts take off their helmets—as Maldano and I had just done—revealing themselves to be not men at all but advanced primates. As a metaphor, it was apropos; we hadn't shaved since well before the moon.

I looked at the pure, perfect sky and its few scattered clouds, like white cotton candy. "Okay. So it wasn't a nuclear exchange or a bolide impact, I think we can safely rule those out." I squinted at the sparse blue dome. "No contrails, no homogenitus, no ash. EMP burst, maybe. But not a large igneous province—Yellowstone, say. Not a caldera. That leaves pandemic—something which had to have raced through the population like wildfire. It's funny. All this time dreaming about home, only to end landing via the Doomsday Protocol."

"Yes, well. Like I said," said Maldano. He looked out over the Gulf of Mexico, which sparkled in the sun. "Could have been a malfunction. All that protocol actually means is that Mission Control hasn't been detected. The fact is–we don't know. It could be that Houston's grid has been down, long enough for emergency power to have dwindled. It's just that–what, what is that? There, low on the horizon."

I followed his gaze to where a handful of queer lights could be seen twinkling amongst the clouds. "I'll be damned if I know. They–they don't look like aircraft. More like navigation buoys, but in the air. I honestly can't tell if they're manmade or not. Look, over there, still more of them." I pointed due south. "It's like someone strung Christmas lights in the sky."

I looked at Maldano and found him already looking at me, sweat beading along his brow. Both of us, I think, were unnerved by the silence, or at least the lack of human activity, and by the crashing drone of the sea. I peered along the waterfront beyond him; it was just us and the bearberry bushes.

"Nobody on the road, nobody on the beach," I said at last, quietly.

The tide rolled in and then out again.

"I feel it in the air; the summer's out of reach," added Maldano.

"Empty lake, empty streets—the sun goes down alone."

"I'm driving by your house—"

And together: "Though I know, *you're not hoome.*"

And we moved out, trudging through the sand toward the boardwalk, singing Don Henley's "The Boys of Summer"—trying, as we walked, to ignore the nearby high rises (hotels, mostly), which looked on in perfect silence, stoic, inert, monolithic, like tombstones.

Unfortunately, by the time we reached the first commercial zone (Cornerstone Plaza of Cocoa Beach), we had no better idea of what had occurred than before, only that the entire suburb had become wild and overgrown—more than what seemed possible in the 21 months we'd been gone—its parks and lawns become mere patches of blowing tundra, its structures choked in moss and vine.

I picked an orange from a nearby tree and rubbed it against my spacesuit. "So here we are—in search of the black swan. The unexpected event that led to—all this." I peeled the fruit as I scanned the shopping center, settling on a storefront with a car crashed through its window. “This–what shall we call it? Death by invasive species.” I split the orange down the middle and tossed him half of it. “This lost country. ‘Untrodden by man, almost unknown to man ... a world tenanted by willows only, and the souls of willows.’”

We raised the portions to our mouths and paused, staring at each other. One of us had to be the Guinee pig, who knew what toxins had bled into the ecosystem, or what poisons had entered the food chain. But which one?

“Algernon Blackwood,” I said, attributing the quote–when it became clear he wasn’t going to waver. *“The Willows.* 1907.”

And then I took a bite–chewing it slowly, as Maldano watched–swallowing, wiping my mouth with a gloved hand. “It’s good. Sweet. Go ahead. Try it.”

He hesitated before peeling off a wedge and placing it in his mouth, at which he closed his eyes and seemed to melt, hanging back his head, working his jaw in a circular motion, reopening his eyes–pausing suddenly.

“What?” I asked. “What is it?”

He tilted his head, peering into the branches. “Isn’t that strange?”

I followed his gaze into the tree but, alas, saw nothing. Which, of course, was precisely the problem; there was nothing–no oranges, no leaves, no uppermost branches, it was as though someone or something had picked the treetop clean.

"Someone has a helluva reach," said Maldano.

I looked around the lot: at the lichen-covered Public Market and the Jersey Mike's Subs with the Prius in its window, at the Vietnamese Nail Salon and the El Buzo Peruvian Restaurant. "We should split up, canvas the area. Make sure–there's nothing else."

"Yeah," said Maldano. "I think you're right."

I headed for the Public Market. "Make a sweep of the strip mall. I'm going to check out that grocery store."

He laughed a little at that–which caused me to pause.

"Orders–Hooper?"

I half-turned, but didn't make eye contact. "Sorry?"

"I mean, in all this? This Big Empty? This 'world tenanted by willows ... and the souls of willows?'"

There was something in his voice. Something subtle, something contentious.

"Call it what you like," I said, and continued toward the market.

I'd barely had time to investigate when I heard him shout, "Hooper! Get out here!"

I looked up from the newspaper I'd picked off the rack—a paper with the headline, DAYS OF DELICATE TERROR: Disappearances, Weird Weather Rock Nation—and tried to triangulate him.

"Outside the Great Clips! Hurry up!"

I folded the paper and took it with me, exiting the building through the jammed-open front doors, and saw him crouched over the asphalt in the corner of the L-shaped shopping center, beneath the Great Clips' cornice. "What is it?" I said. "What did you find?"

He stood and indicated the sidewalk.

I stared at the pavement, which was webbed with roots and lichen, and saw a single shoe lying on its side—a Nike Lebron, which had been stained maroon like the surrounding concrete. More, there was something sticking out of it—two somethings, I realized, broken and brownish-yellow—tibia and fibula bones, obviously, snapped in two midways up their shafts, crawling with maggots and flies.

I used the newspaper to wave away the insects. "Jesus," I said. "What in the hell happened here?"

I scanned the scene, which looked like someone had spilled a 5-gallon bucket of maroon paint (and then flailed around in it), saw an impression the size of a pizza pan in the dried blood. "What the hell is that?"

I glared at Maldano but the bearded astronaut only stared back at me.

I knelt over the impression, or rather the impressions, for there were other, smaller ones next to it–three, to be exact–and studied the configuration.

"This is a–"

"A print, that's right," said Maldano. "Further, I'll characterize it. Or at least what it isn't. It isn't the print of anything that was walking the earth when we left." He added, "It's not that of a bear, for example."

He knelt beside me and indicated the larger impression. "Yuh, see, this would have been left by the lowermost extremity of the metatarsals, the foot bones that connect directly to the tibia and fibula–locked together, for strength." He indicated the smaller ones. "And these, these are the phalanges, or toe bones–see how they're splayed to support the animal's weight? That's because this was a big creature, 7-8 tons, at least. Other than that, they're not so different from our own; here's the proximal phalanx, which is connected to the metatarsal, and the middle phalanx, and the distal phalanx. Or at least that's where they would have been beneath the flesh, which is what left the impress–"

"Stop it," I snapped, and stood abruptly. "Just ... Look. What are you saying?"

"I'm saying this was left by a member of the theropoda clade of the Saurischia order, division Carnosauria." He looked up at me as though it should be obvious. "Whose family was probably—"

I grabbed him by a system umbilical and yanked him to his feet, began shaking him like a ragdoll. "Talk sense, damn you! What are you saying? That whoever that shoe belonged to was attacked by a—by a—"

I paused, trying to get a hold of myself, as his face hovered mere inches from my own. At last I released him and quickly stepped back, breathing heavily, repulsed by my own behavior.

"I—Jesus, I'm sorry. It's just ... it's just that none of this makes any—"

That's when I saw her: like a ghost, or an ashen specter, just staring at me through the glass, through the Great Clips' window, not close to it but much further back, crouched by one of the chairs. That's when I saw her (and she saw me): standing abruptly, stumbling over a broom, regaining her balance in time to bolt for the back door and to disappear into the dark.

"Follow me," I said, rushing to the door, yanking it open. "Hurry!"

Alas, it isn't easy, running in a spacesuit, even if they have been streamlined considerably since Apollo and the shuttle program. The truth of it is that by the time I burst from the building and back into the blinding sun she was already halfway across the lot—and nearing a stand of trees. Indeed, if not for what happened next, I would have surely lost her there; but the bird had other ideas.

The bird. The thing from the sky.

Even now I have a hard time believing it—that such a thing could have ever existed in the first place, much less come to exist again. But the truth of my eyes was undeniable as it swooped in out of nowhere and attacked the girl: its great wings beating furiously as it pecked and stabbed at her with its beak (itself the size of a small kayak) and tore at her with its talons, its eyes flashing malevolently as it attempted to spirit her away but was frustrated repeatedly by her kicking and flailing. And yet it did rise—with her still in its hold—and I sprinted toward them: leaping and grabbing her by the ankles even as the bird lifted us both; absorbing the brunt of the impact when it finally loosened its grip, covering and protecting her as it hovered and pecked and squawked.

Until, finally, the attack had ended—more suddenly even than it had begun—and we were alone (in that moment before Maldano hurried to check on us), at which point I looked at the girl and she looked back—smiling, crying, bleeding profusely—and knew her to be the most beautiful thing on Earth.

As it turned out, she lived at the Discovery Beach Resort, one of the very towers that had looked down on us earlier (and from whose uppermost floor she had watched us touch down). And while I was mystified at first by her choice of residence—there was no electricity to power the elevators, for example—her *modus operandi* quickly became clear: for it was, quite simply, one of the highest and most defensible positions in town (the trek up to the 10th floor alone, especially with her in tow, had more than proven that). What was more, it was high enough from the earth that what had happened below could—if you just listened to the soft jazz sifting from her boombox and tried hard enough—almost be forgotten, at least for a while.

None of which is to say I wasn't shaken as I sat next to her bed and examined the tourniquet on her arm—which we'd fashioned out of a haircutter's drape while still at the Great Clips—and worried over the appearance of the wound, which had developed red streaks around it and was oozing clearish fluid.

"Well now, here comes Doctor Number Two. I shall need your name as well, sir," she said, and smiled, toothily, earnestly.

"Hooper," I said. "Captain Glenn Hooper. Bluespace Aeronautics."

She saluted sharply with her good arm and lowered her voice. "Pleased to meet you, Captain Hooper."

I chuckled in spite of everything. "Just Glenn," I said.

"'Just Glenn'–he says," she quipped. She lifted her chin and arched her back, to gaze out the window behind her. "And I'll tell you the same thing I told him. Ain't no one who's been to Mars is *'just'* anything."

She yawned and stretched in the thin nightshirt and I looked away. "Well–thank you. But we were just doing our job. I'm sure you had one that was just as important. Didn't you, Miss–?"

"Cunningham. Rachael Cunningham." She rolled her head to look at me. "I was a teacher; an adjunct. Comparative politics. Political methodology. That sort of thing."

Her eyes were cow-brown with emerald highlights.

"That sounds interesting, indeed," I said–calmly, clinically. It seemed especially important to be so; I wasn't sure why. *"And* necessary."

She *hrmphed.* "In the age of Tucker? What did it matter?"

She was referring, of course, to Donald J. Tucker, the 45th President of the United States.

I looked at my moonboots, knowing I should let her rest but not wanting to go. "Whatever happened to him, you think? In this—this Flashback, as you called it."

She faced the ceiling as though in deep thought. "Who knows. He's probably golfing in an underground bunker somewhere. It's funny; I saw a caravan of trucks come through town just the other day, flying his flag—like their own little mobile nation-state."

She lolled her head to look at me and we laughed, softly, quietly.

At length she said, "You must be terribly uncomfortable in that, your spacesuit. You should go check the other units, see if there's anything to wear. I've pretty much cleaned out the women's necessities, but there should be plenty of men's clothing; not to mention razors and shave cream. I'll be fine, really."

I stood reluctantly and moved to go, but paused in the doorway. "That wound, you know, it has me concerned. You'll need to be monitored, closely. Is there a thermometer?"

She shook her head.

"Yeah, well. We'll look for one."

"There's a pharmacy at Cornerstone Plaza, just a few blocks away. You can take my Kawasaki; the key's on the mantle." She laughed. "But go gently—the thing's 46 years old."

I must have grinned. "You don't say? I had a '78. KZ400. It was red."

"So's this one." She seemed to think about it. "Isn't that strange?"

"I guess something's just click into place like that," I said, and regretted it immediately. "Listen. You get some sleep, you hear?"

"I will, if you doctors will leave me alone." She smiled, toothily, earnestly.

"You know it's funny," she added, as I was closing the door. "I used to lay awake at night and wonder if I'd ever have anyone to talk to again. And now I've got two—more than any woman could need."

I stared at her through the crack in the door, unsure how to respond. Then I eased the door gently closed and went to join Maldano on the patio.

We settled into a routine—Maldano taking the morning while I looked in on her in the afternoon—ending our days in deck chairs while drinking whiskey sours and gazing at the Sargasso Sea (and also our starship, which stood sentinel below us like a Minuteman missile). None of which changed the fact that she seemed to be getting worse, not better, or that, in spite of her denials, she appeared to have lost mobility in her hand and fingers—a sure sign of infection, at least with an animal bite. The fact was she needed antibiotics, and soon. The fact was we'd need to return to the shopping plaza at Cocoa Beach.

"Yes, but. With a pair of .22 calibers weapons? How is that a good idea?"

Maldano was skeptical.

I thought about the weapons in question, which were the only ones she had: a Rimfire Pistol and a Model 60 Rifle, both of them well-maintained. "I'm not seeing that we have much of a choice—are you? You heard what she said: the gun stores have been emptied. But you've felt her lymph nodes, her forehead—she's burning up. No. We can't wait on this, Mark. It's going to have to be done. I say first thing in the morning."

He swirled the liquor in his glass, appearing to think about it. "I guess it's hard to say no to the last woman on Earth."

"There's others," I said, and took a drink. "People have survived." I gazed at the queer lights as they shifted and pulsed amongst the clouds and the whiskey burned my chest. "As for how many ..." I looked across at him and his loud Hawaiian shirt. "You're right, of course. She might as well be. Who knows."

"Who knows," he said, and took a drink.

We watched as the gray waves crashed and the tide rolled in and out, as the light itself began to fade.

"Our Lady of the Flashback!" he exclaimed at last, and raised his glass to the sky. "This—this Dinosaur Apocalypse; this Time Storm which has cleansed the world." He swirled the glass, sloshing whiskey. "Our brown-eyed, toothy Galatea; our Aphrodite on a scallop shell. The veritable Eve to these two Adams."

He swung his glass close to mine, as though he wished to toast. "To starting again; and to being home. 'Muses no more what ere ye be, in fancy's pleasures roam; but sing (by truth inspir'd) wi' me, the pleasures of a home." He rattled his glass. "Eh?"

I hesitated before meeting him, I'm not sure why. "John Clare. *The Village Minstrel.* 1821." I tapped his glass (a little harder than I intended). "Scoal."

"Mm," he said, and drained his glass. "She'd like that, I bet. Some poetry. I've been reading to her from the *Bhagavad Gita*—but it's slow going. Found it wedged in amongst all those Eckhart Tolle books in the hall."

I paused, looking at him. "You—you've been *reading* to her?"

"Well, sure. Beats all that small talk and temperature taking you've been smothering her with." He laughed. "Woman does not heal by bread alone, mein Captain. Nor does lamb always trump harvest—regardless of what it says in the Bible. She's smart; I treat her like it. I think she misses teaching. Terribly."

I stared at the lights in the sky, wondering again if they were intelligently directed or some kind of natural phenomenon. "I didn't realize it was a competition," I said, absently.

"Neither did Abel," he jibed, and shoved me in the arm.

I drained my glass as he looked out over the ocean and the silence reasserted itself. "But then, everything is, I suppose," he said, after seeming to think about it. "I mean, isn't that what's going on out there, right now—a competition for survival? For reproduction?" He chuckled, softly, and with little discernible humor. "Sharks versus marlins; monster birds versus women—she said it was a quetzalcoatlus—Tucker fanatics versus, who knows?"

I looked at our starship: at its stainless-steel hull which shown cool and blue in the building's dim shadow. "No. No, I don't think so," I said. "We've

... transcended all that, to some extent. I mean, *look at it,* Mark. Look at what we've accomplished."

He followed my gaze, holding his glass loosely, tenuously, his eyes blurry and red. "It–it looks like a giant hard-on," he said, and tittered. He began looking for the bottle. "Or maybe a middle finger. Like a big 'Fuck You' to God."

I watched as he stumbled through the sliding glass doors into the kitchen. "You should lay off that," I said. "We've got a big day tomorrow."

But by then he was retching into the sink and I was alone, just looking at my empty glass, wondering, a little amused: Did he see himself as Abel? Or did he see himself as Cain?

I thought about Rachael, sleeping in her thin nightshirt, having more than any woman could need; and about myself, and how I saw myself. And then I dozed, dreaming of home–which was curious, since, like Maldano, I had never really had one (hence one of the reasons we were chosen for Mars). A dream which soon gave way to the faint smell of blood and an impulse I could not define; and of gliding through dark water–stealthily, surefootedly–like a predator, or a wraith.

I'm still not sure where it came from, the ramosaurus, as I called it (a kind of allosaurus, but with little ram-like horns on each side of its head), although I'd hazard a guess, based on its later behavior, that it had been watching us for a some time; since well before I'd started the Kawasaki's engine and kicked it into 1st gear–tearing up the street like gangbusters as Maldano hung on for dear life and the carnosaur pursued, chasing us all the way to the shopping center, where we quickly climbed off and rushed in.

"Get back," I shouted at Maldano, "Get back!" –even as the animal's snout darted between the doors and stopped; suddenly, abruptly, jarring the metal framework, cracking the glass into spiderwebs.

"It's okay," gasped Maldano–breathing heavily, holding his chest. "It's okay." He laughed suddenly, euphorically. "Ha! Its head is too big for its own good."

We watched as it struggled and gnashed its teeth–its dark tail whipping back and forth outside, its eyes close to the glass. "It's all those denticles and jaw muscles," I said, finally. "Cost of doing business, I guess."

"Apex predator's burden," said Maldano, and indicated the door to the pharmacy, which was lazed open.

We went in even as the ramosaur withdrew, opening and closing its little claws–shaking itself off.

"Let's hope it doesn't get the idea to use those horns," said Maldano. He handed me a green plastic bag. "We're looking for Amoxicillin and Penicillin. Also Doxycycline, Metronidazole, Clindamycin. If you see Dicloxacillin, grab that too. And painkillers. Ibuprofen and Tylenol."

He went to the glass partition which separated the pharmacy from the rest of the store and peered out.

"What are you doing?" I asked.

"Making sure there's no light pouring in anywhere, no opening. Nothing that *thing* can get in through. So far, so good." He took out his flashlight and pressed its lens against the pane. "And also that there's nothing in here with us. I don't trust this glass."

I pulled the blinds to let in more light–in time to see the ramosaur's tail disappear behind the Holiday Inn next door, followed by its head peeking around the corner–cautiously, stealthily. "Our friend doesn't give up easily ..."

I turned to look at Maldano, saw him still peering into the darkened store. "We're going to have to ditch the bike and slip out the back," I said. "How's it looking?"

He began to back away from the glass, slowly, blindly, as though he were in a daze. "I–I can't do it. I'm sorry."

I watched as he drew the pistol from his belt and chambered a round, then pointed it, waveringly, at the partition.

"What the hell are you talking about?" I took a step toward him. "Maldano. What are you talking about?"

"We—we have to go. *Now.* I—*I* have to go. Out the front doors. Out—"

"What is it, Mark? What do you see?" I shoved past him and put my own light to the window, squinting as my eyes adjusted, thinking I saw something move.

And I did. I *did* see something move, several somethings, a hundred—a *thousand,* maybe more. For the store was crawling with centipedes, *huge* ones, and ones still larger than those, ones ranging from 3 feet to 8 feet and some several feet across, ranging in color from lime green to faded salmon, from drab brown to sickly ochre, all of them winding and weaving, gliding on scurrying legs, flopping and scrambling over themselves, glistening like moist, wet clay.

"We have to go!" he shouted, dropping his gun, and bolted for the door.

"Wait! Maldano! It isn't safe!"

I moved to follow him but froze, adjusting the rifle sling, looking at the shelves and shelves of medicines. Rachael. She was counting on us.

Rachael in her thin white nightshirt–in her room full of soft jazz and incense; in her tower by the sea. Rachael who was not simply a woman but something akin to *home* itself.

I rushed to the shelves and began searching for Penicillin, for Doxycycline and Metronidazole, for painkillers of any kind. Searched for them and found some, even as the motorcycle sputtered to life.

"Hurry up!" shouted Maldano. "We have to go! Now!"

But I couldn't, of course; I had to gather the medicines. I had to save Galatia, our Aphrodite on a scallop shell. Had to think of home and a final place to rest. "It's not safe, damn you!" I cried, sweeping pill bottles with my arm, filling the plastic bag. "That thing, it's still out there!"

I gazed out the window at the Holiday Inn, saw the creature creeping forward with its body slung low, intently, single-mindedly, like a wolf or a great cat. I jerked to look at Maldano and saw that he too was aware of it; that he had apprehended the animal and was trying to figure out the motorcycle's gears–that he was kicking down into 1st, which was correct, and releasing the clutch. And then he leapt forward, suddenly, and travelled about 50 feet–before the engine stalled and he was immobile again.

I dropped the bag and unslung the rifle, smashed the window with its butt. Then I aimed and ground the scope, sighting the dinosaur between its eyes.

I must have gone into what they call *hyperfocus,* because it gets foggy after that. All I know for certain is that I understood in that moment what was required to move forward; that Eve would need her Adam and that I would need to choose survival, for this above everything was what the world now demanded. And I knew, also, that while a .22 caliber round was unlikely to stop the creature, a fresh kill would surely give it pause, enough, perhaps, for me to escape through the back with the medicines—even if it meant running straight through the centipedes.

I lowered my sights to Maldano, who tried to kickstart the bike and failed, then raised to try again.

It would have to be fresh. It would have to be alive.

And then I fired—once, twice. A third time. Knowing the battery was directly beneath the seat. Knowing it was shielded only by a thin layer of plastic.

Knowing it had exploded only when the cover blew off and white smoke started to billow—after which, shaken and confused, Maldano turned to look at me—pitifully, mournfully; resigned—and the animal pounced, pinning him to the pavement like a moth on cork, clamping its jaws about his head and chest, pulling him asunder as though he were full of blood red centipedes.

I am running, running along the back of the strip mall, gripping the medicine bag in one hand and the Model 60 rifle in the other, trying to get home. I run the entire two blocks to the Discovery Beach Resort–my heart thumping in my chest, my eyes stinging with something like tears–until I gain the door and go in–pausing only briefly to catch my shuddering breath; beginning the 10-story climb as though I were scaling Babel itself.

When I get to the unit it is dark, the generator sitting silently out on the deck (the door to which is open), the curtains rustling in the breeze. But there is no time to waste, none to delay, and I quickly gain the bedroom–at which I realize the bed is empty and she is no longer there, the sheets left in a jumbled mess, the draperies blowing as if to accentuate the solitude.

I look for her for hours, all throughout the building, kicking in doors which were previously unexplored, searching the utility rooms and common areas and dining accommodations, doubting my very grip on reality; until at last I burst through a door and find myself on the boardwalk, back on the beach, feeling cold, all of a sudden, and shivering, feeling as though my flesh were thin as paper. Feeling, for a reason I cannot explain, that I must return—to the starship, of course, the only home I have ever known, but also to myself, who would never have slain his own friend, his own brother—no matter the madhouse the world has become, or the perceived stakes of any given situation. Until I find myself stumbling from the boardwalk onto the beach—and across the sand like a drunkard—collapsing at last at the base of our starship, raising a hand, which trembles, to its steel.

That's when I remember them, the queer lights in the sky. That's when I slide to the sand as though having no bones—gazing at them disoriented, knowing them to be alive. Suspecting, in my heart, that we have somehow been judged, and that by doing what I've done they have judged me again. Fearing, in my mind, that Rachael has never existed, or, if she has, has done so only at their pleasure, their humor. Their terrible intent. At which I begin to crawl upon the sand like a snake, gripping handfuls of granules and coughing and gasping as though dying, seeking the edge of the world and the nightmare; groping for a way back into reality itself.

After which I stand, teeteringly, and stumble on, banished and shunned, naked and alone, bearing the mark of Cain.

Burn

Because the windows were bulletproof, it all had to come out through the main entrance, and that included the grand piano in the Entrance Hall—which we wheeled recklessly against the doorframe before upending it with a huff and shoving it down the stairs, where it sounded briefly, chaotically, as it impacted each step. By then I was leaning on one side of the door while Fiona leaned on the other, looking on: at our friends as they started busting up the instrument below with bats and feet and sledgehammers, but also at the overgrown North Lawn of the White House and its spitting, crackling bonfire; at the tricked out Hondas and Toyotas as they continued pouring onto the field and bringing more—more beer kegs and more gasoline, more children of the Flashback, more us.

"Look at it, big sister," I said, finding her already staring at me in the flickering semi-dark, "It's like poetry, I swear."

"Green Room," she answered calmly, seeming almost to smolder. "And stop calling me that."

My eyes flicked up and down her body—something they'd been doing a lot of lately—but I don't think she noticed. Of course she was right; a lot had changed since our first burn—not the least of which was my voice—and calling her that no longer seemed appropriate. She, too, had changed—becoming less like a big sister (or even a mother) and more like an equal, even if, at 19, she still had a good 4 years on me.

"Okay, babe," I said, winking at her. I kicked the pedestal and candelabra next to me over with a resounding crash. "So let's do it."

And we went to work, Fiona pulling down the pictures and the red and green curtains while I took my bat to the china cabinet—smashing the glass as though it were a thin layer of ice, sending shards of it flying, bludgeoning the green plates and gold leafed vases like piñatas, like the shattered skulls of imagined enemies, until 243 years of history lay a glistening wreck at my feet—just so much broken detritus to be burned with the rest; just so much dust and memory to be erased and finally forgotten. At which I looked at Fiona and she looked back, smiling, her teeth large and slightly crooked, carnivorous—because it was a pleasure to burn, an ecstasy to burn.

By the time we rejoined the party, the bonfire was licking at the boughs of the maple trees and the staging had been erected for Calvin's speech—staging he was already ascending, gripping the rungs with one hand while holding a rolled up document—or documents—in the other, the firelight reflecting off his glasses.

"So what's he going to talk about?" I asked Fiona, heaving one of the two chairs I'd brought onto the fire—its red upholstery going up like dry paper, creating plumes of black smoke.

"How should I know? He's barely said two words to me since North Carolina." She pitched the framed pictures she was carrying—one of a dude she'd called Jimmy Carter—onto the roaring heap. "Look, Leif. I know he's something of a hero to you ... but you don't know him like I do. And I'm telling you, his heart's no longer in this. The Burning. It hasn't been since Georgia. At least."

I threw the other chair onto the pyre. "But it was his idea in the first place—wasn't it? Isn't that what you said—"

"I've said a lot of things," she snapped, and used her whole body to throw the second picture. "People change, Leif. At least some do. Others just get old."

I paused, thinking about that. Had something happened between them, like a fight? What did that mean, 'Others just get old?'"

"Okay, wild children, listen up!" cried Calvin from the top of the platform—and waved the rolled up documents to get everyone's attention. "Hear, hear! You're having *way* too much fun."

It took a minute but eventually the car stereos and loose chatter diminished and the silence reasserted itself—or nearly so, for the fire continued to crack and to pop and to roar like a veritable furnace.

"But then, why else would God have invented adolescence—if not to have fun?"

Hoots and cheers, whistles and applause.

"And that we have had. From Austin to Baton Rouge and Jackson to Montgomery, from Atlanta to Raleigh and Norfolk to Richmond ... to come at last to Washington, and the seat of Old Power itself. To come at last to the very pinnacle of what we set out to do—which was to loot and burn every vestige of what had come before; every deed and every banknote, every binding contract and article of law, and to cede them back to whatever chaos must ultimately rule our lives."

He looked out over us, his friends, his people, and seemed to reflect. "And yet I wonder—what remains of the old world and the old laws to douse and burn? I mean, besides these ..." He lifted the rolled papers above his head, inciting raucous applause. "These relics of a bygone age– which Leif and Fiona have so brazenly liberated? Well, I tell you, there is one thing–but we'll save that for later, when they return ..."

I looked at Fiona and she looked back. Were we going back to the Archives?

"For now, let us commend these, one U.S. Constitution and one Declaration of Independence, to the fires of a New World–a world as young and savage and beautiful as we are, for it has yet to see even its 30th month, just as we have yet to see our 30th year. And afterward, afterward, I'll have a special announcement. Right now it's time to party; and to dance on the grave of that which is old and dead–and which never served us anyway. *Salud!"*

"Salud!" echoed the crowd, raising their plastic cups.

And then he was unfurling the documents and dropping them into the fire, which hissed and popped and seemed almost alive, and Fiona and I were shoving our way through the crowd–both of us, I think, wondering where we were being sent, and more importantly, what this 'special announcement' might be.

"Babe," said Calvin, descending the ladder, and I looked away as he and Fiona embraced (briefly), I'm not sure why.

"Got another job for you two—if you're up to it."

"If we're up to it," said Fiona, and laughed, at which there was an awkward silence I didn't understand. "I know: You want us to take a group of bad apples and put down the Norsemen. Am I right?"

The Norsemen were the older group whose territory we'd violated in order to access the White House and National Mall—and who were bound to cause us trouble if we didn't leave soon.

"Wrong. I want you to go to the National Museum and liberate the Star-Spangled Banner—the flag, not the song—and bring it here to be burned."

Fiona shot me a glance. "He's a vandal, Leif, not a fighter."

"I'm not a killer, if that's what you mean," he retorted, then turned away and watched the fire, hands on his hips. "Nor will I let any of us be. I mean, if I've said it once I'll say it again: this isn't about bloodshed. It's not even about rebellion. It's more about ..." He paused—as though saying anything else could only lead to regret.

"I thought it was about nothing," said Fiona, softly. "That that was its beauty—it was wildness for the sake of wildness. Passion for the sake of passion.

Isn't that what you said?" She laughed with surprising bitterness. "Different context, I guess."

"It was about filling the nothing," he said, still facing away. "And letting go. Until ... But then—you haven't had to think about any of that ... have you? No one's made you king."

"And cue the Messiah Complex," fumed Fiona, which I took as my cue to leave; to give them space—to let them hash it out, whatever it was—after which I wandered over to one of the kegs and filled a cup, reckoning that next to a roaring fire wasn't the best place to keep beer—because it tasted like piss, literally. Nor did I stop at one but downed three in rapid succession, wondering what Calvin had meant by 'filling the nothing' and 'letting go,' and about being king—not to mention starting a sentence with 'until' ... but never finishing it.

And I guess I must have stood there for a while, because I distinctly recall watching the same group of teens—their arms laden with destruction—moving back and forth between the fire and the White House—the fucking White House!—to the point that I began feeling shitty about what we'd done; and even a little sick to my stomach. But then Fiona returned jingling Calvin's keys and we were firing up his Mustang convertible, and the next thing I remember she was piloting us down 14th Street NW past buildings with Doric columns (now choked in prehistoric ivy) and a pair of grazing stegosaurs and at least one giant millipede; all the way to Constitution Avenue and the National Museum; which I took special note of only because I was trying not to look at her body—something she noticed, I'm sure, but didn't seem to mind—because she just glanced at me beneath the blood red sky and smiled—toothily. Carnivorously.

It was the sort of thing you had to actually *see;* up close, personal—as up close and personal as the glass would allow, anyway—to fully appreciate; to fully understand that this was *it,* the flag that inspired the national anthem, the actual Fort McHenry garrison flag, a thing more than 40 feet high and maybe 30 feet long, laying at an angle in a climate-controlled black room, or a room that *had* been climate-controlled, until the Flashback, until the lights had gone out from Anchorage to Miami.

"Oh, say can you see," I sang, moving my flashlight over the material, which was tattered and torn, "By the dawn's early light ..."

I grinned and trailed off, letting the silence take control, letting the room buzz, and we just stood there.

"What so proudly we hailed," sang Fiona at length, her voice cracking a little, "at the twilight's last gleaming." She took a breath in the dark. "Whose broad stripes and bright stars ... through the perilous fight ... O'er the ramparts we watched—were so gallantly streaming ..."

Then, together: "And the rocket's red glare, the bombs bursting in air, gave proof through the night ... that our flag was still there." We both took a breath. "Oh, say does that star-spangled *ba-anner* yet wave ... o'er the *land* of the free ... and the *home* ... of the ... brave."

And again there was a silence, as perfect and deep as anything I'd ever experienced, either then or since.

"Fuck," I said.

"Yeah," said Fiona. "Fuck."

I looked at the sparse starfield illuminated in her beam.

"They're all gone," I said, and lowered my flashlight. "Everyone who ever touched this. Those who first sowed it; those who stood in its shadow. Those who built this building to preserve it—all gone."

"Yeah," whispered Fiona. "It's just us."

"I don't know, big sis—I mean 'babe.' But do you ever wonder if—like, we're doing the right thing?"

"No."

"Okay. Well. Why is that, exactly?"

"Because there is no right thing. I mean, maybe there was ... before the universe just—went bugfuck. Before everyone just vanished. But now? What's right and what's wrong, Leif? I mean, what could possibly make any difference—one way or the other?"

"I don't know. It just seems that, like—"

"You're sounding like Calvin; don't go there. Because, I'm telling you, he's not who you think he is. Not anymore. He's—"

"Evolving?"

"Aging. Just aging. There's a difference."

"It's going to happen," I said. "We can't stay teenagers for—"

"Can't we?" She shook her head. "Maybe you don't see yourself ... but I do. See you, that is. And let me tell you—*you're a fire.*" She touched my hand where it gripped the sledgehammer. "And fires need to keep moving, keep consuming," She raised my arm gently, assuredly, until I dropped my flashlight completely and took the hammer in both hands. "... or they burn out."

And then I swung, harder than I ever had before, harder even than when I'd destroyed the china hutch, punching a white crater into the glass as big my head, causing cracks to spread out in rings, like a contagion, I thought, or a cancer, until I swung again and the head of the hammer smashed clean through, enough so that I had to fight to pull it back out, after which Fiona joined in and we smashed through the glass together, not all at once but blow after blow, until the bitter shards lay all around us and we fell to the flag's faded cloth, kissing and groping each other with abandon, unfastening and working off each other's clothes, fucking like it was the end of the world, which of course it was—consuming each other like paper in fire.

It goes without saying that I was driving too fast; I was 15 and had just gotten laid. Add to that my inexperience—and a spike strip laid across the road—and, well, you probably have some idea how we ended up in the fountain of the Ronald Reagan Building with Old Glory folded up and sticking out of the trunk. All I know for certain is that we were both injured, Fiona seriously—to the extent that the blood from her head had fouled her left eye and she couldn't stop shaking; which is how I noticed the figures approaching us from behind (I saw them in the rearview mirror when I removed Calvin's doo-rag, to stop her bleeding).

"Fiona, listen—we—we gotta get out of here. Can you walk?"

"What is it?" she asked, weakly, deliriously, looking around like a blind person (which I suppose she was), bleeding profusely.

I squinted at the figures—there were more of them now—saw long beards and jackboots; rifles, riot gear, motorcycle helmets to which horns had been attached.

"Norsemen," I said. "Lots of them. Hold on."

I threw open my door and went around, noticing how exposed we were, how exposed the entrance to the building was.

"I'm going to put you across my back, okay? Just hang on."

"Okay."

"Here we go—"

And then I heaved her across my back and we went, hustling up 14th Street NW even as the Norsemen opened fire and the pavement sparked all around us—all the way to something called the M.I.M. Museum, the door of which I kicked in awkwardly before carrying Fiona up a flight of steps and laying her before a giant mural, after which I collapsed against the nearby wall—the window of which promptly exploded.

"Fuck!" I cursed, lying flat on my stomach, then crawled through the glass to Fiona where I shielded her lithe body with my own.

"It's okay, we're okay," I said quickly, even as she started to hyperventilate. "We're fine. They don't know we're not armed–they don't know we're not armed. They're not going to come in. Not yet."

I wrapped her in my arms and held her tight, even as the other windows were blown out and glass rained down. And then, just as suddenly as it had begun, it was over; at least for the moment–after which I lifted my head, slowly, cautiously, and listened.

Nothing. A squawk of a pterodactyl, maybe, way off in the distance.

"Leif?" managed Fiona, groggily. "Are you there?"

I squeezed her tightly, stunned that she couldn't feel it. *"Shh-shhh,"* I said, stroking her hair, which was matted with blood, kissing her forehead.

At last a voice called, "We just want the girl. Give us the girl; vacate the House and the Mall, and we're done here. All right?"

I held Fiona close trying to still her trembling–realizing, in the process, that I was trembling myself. *"Shhh*–it's okay," I said, finding her hand, enveloping it in my own. "Everything is going to be okay."

"Aww, you're sweet," she said, her voice faint, papery. "But it's not. It never has been. You know that. Even before the Flashback."

"Shhh," I repeated, and diverted my eyes to the mural, which depicted, in stark black and white, seemingly all the atrocities human beings had ever committed–most of which I was unfamiliar with, the Holocaust and Hiroshima being obvious exceptions.

"They're right, you know," she said, softly, having followed my gaze. "The lights in the clouds. The shapes ... in that beautiful borealis, that came with the Flashback. They're right about us."

But I only stared at the painting, at the depictions of medieval torture and Mayan beheadings, at the lifeless, flattened cities and mounds of emaciated corpses, like driftwood; at the piles of skulls and perfect, white tombstones extending forever.

"... Right to have–how would they say it? To have 'cancelled' us." She laughed a little, which became a series of jagged coughs. "And Calvin ... Calvin is wrong. About you. About me. About everyone."

She shifted her head slightly, looking at the whole mural. "We ... we were *meant* to burn."

I angled my head to look at her; at the dark, smoldering eyes, the large, slightly mis-aligned teeth, even as she exhaled in a long, rattling breath, and just shrunk–like a bag with all the air sucked out; like a marionette lowered to the floor in an unrecognizable heap. After which I pressed my cheek to her own and just stayed that way, although for how long I couldn't possibly say. All I know is that I was 'awakened' by gunshots, by the *crack-crack* of small arms, followed by screaming; screaming and the instantly recognizable growls of dinosaurs—big ones, by the sound of it—which itself gave way to silence ... at which I knew, with a mixture of relief and anger (because it was too late for Fiona anyway), that the Norsemen were no more.

By the time I'd walked all the way back to the White House and the North Lawn—carrying Fiona's body on my shoulders—Calvin's announcement was well underway, although it came to an abrupt halt when I appeared near the scaffold and laid her at its feet; after which there were gasps followed by a hushed silence—that is, save for the ubiquitous crackling of the fire.

When at last Calvin spoke, he did so as someone who had already resigned himself to the harsh reality of her death, asking only if she had suffered, to which I responded, "No," and then inviting me to join him on the platform, which I did, climbing the rungs and taking his offered hand until we stood together over the crowd and the roaring pyre and he had turned to address his audience again.

"And so it goes," he said, simply, giving the moment time to breathe, allowing everyone to catch their breath, until someone unexpectedly shouted, "How did she die?" —at which he turned to me, humbly, impotently, I thought, and indicated I should step forward; which I did, stepping to the very edge of the platform and looking down at the flames and the upturned faces, liking the way it felt, liking the way it made my blood race and seemed to snap everything into focus, liking the sense of power and purpose.

"Norsemen," I said, bluntly, after which, having been a student of Calvin since before puberty, meaning I'd idolized him and observed him carefully in the hopes that I might one day be like him, I let the moment breathe—until, finally, I added, "They laid a trap ... and we blundered into it. And then they issued an ultimatum: Leave now. Leave, or die."

"Fuck them!" barked someone almost immediately, and was quickly joined by others—all of whom felt that retaliation should be swift as it was lethal.

"We outnumber them five to one! I say we do it now, while it's dark, and we have the element of surprise!"

At which Calvin quickly tugged me back and we changed places, so that I was standing behind him as he said, "Now wait just a minute, gang, just hold that line of thought. Because, see, the thing is, we *are* in their territory. All right? They warned us and we–well, we rightfully ignored them, because, as you say," He pointed at one of the teenagers, "We outnumbered them. By about five to one, as you say. But that's because we–we had a *job* to do. We had to come here and ... and burn what remained of the Old World, the old ways. But the Burning is done, don't you understand? We've done what we set out to do, we've burned it *fucking all!"*

He looked left and right quickly, as though to fan the flames–taking them all in, seeking to build momentum. When no one spoke up he said, "And that's why I think it's time to ... to consider a new way. A new paradigm, as they say. A new, well, a new purpose. A way–"

"Our purpose is to burn!" shouted someone near the front, an expression which was met with cheers and sustained applause, and at least one horse whistle.

"Yes! Yes, it is!" Calvin shouted back, and hastened to add, "And so you have! So you have. And so very, very brightly, I might add. But there comes a time when ... when Time itself–begins to *mutate.* When your mind and your body begin to change, to *evolve.*"

"It's called getting old!" someone shouted, and was met by laughter.

"It's also called adapting; just bending ever so slightly so that instead of blowing you over the wind becomes an *ally,* a source of energy, and a renewable one at that. What I'm saying is ... the Burn is over. That the fields have been thoroughly cleansed and prepped. And that it's time to ... to build again. It's time to re-learn farming, irrigation, how to brew beer, for God's sake! Because the keg–the keg eventually runs out. And that's because what we're doing here isn't sustainable. It–it never was. *But.* But. You wanted a leader ... and somehow you found me. And so it was up to me in those first dark days to lift you up and to bolster your spirits, to channel your energy, to keep you busy and just get you through it." He sounded fatherly, patriarchal. "To help you let go of what was–and will never be again."

He turned toward me suddenly, I don't know why. "So ... no. There will be no retaliation. Not against the Norsemen, nor any other group. And there will be no more destruction." And then he held out his hand–I'm still not sure why–and I just looked at it; wondering if he knew, somehow–if he had intuited it. That Fiona and I had lain together;

that I was beginning to doubt his wisdom and his leadership, just as she had. That's when I noticed his hand was shaking slightly, as I had seen the hands of the very old and infirm do, and when I looked to his face I could see it—the age, the wear and tear, the lines just beginning to form around his eyes and his mouth, the hint of darkness just above his cheeks. But then he shook his hand as though urging me to take it and I did—grasping it firmly, assuredly—and we pulled each other into an embrace, a right bear hug, slapping each other on the back, seeming to acknowledge what we had in common, which, I was beginning to suspect, was a penchant for leadership. And Fiona.

But then I lifted my gaze over his shoulder—following the billowing embers, as I recall—and saw that great and terrible borealis in the sky and the dark shapes within it; saw the lights which shifted and bled in and out of each other and the alien colors which were not colors at all as we knew them but rather facets of some strange and inconceivable prism, and knew, even before I looked, that I would see those same colors in the eyes of the children below—the lost children, the children of the Flashback—just as I had seen them in the eyes of the dinosaurs which now ruled the earth. And more, that if I were to look, I'd see them in my own. And that's when I slid the shard of glass out of my back pocket (the one I'd kept as a keepsake after making love to Fiona) and, clasping it in both hands—so that it cut me deep before anyone else—drove it into Calvin's lower back.

At which Time stopped. It didn't mutate; it didn't evolve and transform—it just stopped; for I, and I alone, had stopped it. And then I was jerking Calvin against me, violently, brutally, again and again, sinking the shard deep into his flesh, using it to impale his spine, until he began coughing up blood—which gurgled darkly in the twilight and for the briefest of moments made one giant bubble—before releasing him completely and letting him fall backward into the fire, where he impacted like a fresh log, causing embers to explode upward, and began screaming—hideously, obscenely. Briefly.

"Salud!" cried everyone below at once, raising their fists in solidarity, even as I looked at the sky yet again and considered what I saw there, and what I had seen of myself; as I considered what I had seen in the M.I.M. Museum and in Fiona's dying eyes.

You wanted a fresh start, I said to them, the lights, the shapes *within* the lights. *You wanted to cleanse away the old. Let us help you.*

And then I looked at my friends, at my people, my *tribe,* seeing the Flashback in their eyes and knowing, at last, that this was its final expression; that we were meant to burn and to be burned, to end everything we'd ever touched; to end it all and to finally end ourselves. To just walk into the fire and close the book for good. To fertilize the fields for whatever was to come next.

To burn and to burn brightly.

To burn and to be burned, briefly.

Elegy

Okay, easy does it. Just nock your arrow–easy, easy, it's going to click–now put it in the rest ...

I looked at the allosaur as it fed, there in the slim shadow of the Mirage's entry arch, in the shimmering heat of Lost Vegas, and drew back the string–finding my anchor (which was just under my right ear), aligning the peephole with my sights.

Easy, easy ...

I stabilized the grip between my thumb and forefinger, sighting the area between the arms, the claws of which were covered in gore.

Great Spirit, thank you for sharing with me your glorious nature and abundant wildlife–

There was a *thwish* as a I released the arrow.

Grant me always wisdom and respect in its pursuit–

Which struck the taupe-colored animal with a dull thump, causing it to rear up like a stallion, baying and squealing, barking at the sky.

And keep me ever humble in the harvest–

I nocked and released two more bolts, embedding them into its chest, into its great, beating heart.

So that I may be worthy of my place on this earth. Amen.

And it fell, the fast-acting microraptor venom locking its jaw, paralyzing its limbs, so that it squirmed briefly upon its belly before solidifying like stone (as though it had gazed upon Medusa herself) and lay still, at which Kesabe leapt from the palm bushes and bound toward it, barking and wagging his tail, and I followed, grateful for the meat yet distressed by the loss of the arrows—which I knew would never be recovered—and overall preoccupied enough that I didn't even notice the girl standing just beyond the kill—until she yelped once, taking me in, and bolted out of sight down S. Las Vegas Blvd; after which I heard a small engine sputter to life and begin to rev.

"Sic, Kesabe!" I barked, for she was the first person we'd seen since San Diego—but the Dutch Shepherd was already on it, leaping over the allosaur's tail and sprinting after her even as I shouldered the compound bow and fetched Blucifer, whom I mounted quickly, gracelessly, before cracking the reins and giving chase.

And then there we were, she on her motor scooter (which sputtered and whined and left a trail of oily blue smoke) while we pursued, weaving between empty cars, maneuvering around stalled buses, racing down the Strip past Harrah's and Caesar's and the rows of transplanted palm trees—all the way to Planet Hollywood and a wide set of stairs (which she attempted to navigate but failed); all the way until Kesabe fell upon her like a threshing machine and I at last trotted to a halt, calling him off.

Fortunately, she hadn't been hurt, at least not seriously: she had a few nicks from Kesabe's teeth—a given—along with some minor cuts and bruises, but that was it. She was, however, pinned beneath her scooter; a circumstance she could do virtually nothing about—considering Kesabe's close proximity.

"Bastard!" she cursed—her voice full of venom—and spat at me. "What do you want?"

I recoiled as though slapped in the face, as though her small voice were instead the loudest thing in the world (which, at that time and place, now that I think about it, it *was).* And then the silence reasserted itself, as total and sublime as anything since Death Valley—only worse, for I now had something to compare it to—and because I was a man, and alone, with no rules to govern me, and because I'd heard nothing but death birds since the Cleveland National Forest, I decided I would not just slake my curiosity and let her go (who she was, where she was from, what did she know) but that in fact I would keep her, as a bound prisoner if necessary. In part this was to protect her, for she wouldn't last long with no weapons and no guile, but mainly it was for myself. Because, having heard her voice once, I intended to keep hearing it.

I *needed* to keep hearing it.

By the time I'd established a camp in the covered breezeway of the Luxor obelisk—"Cleopatra's Needle" it was called, at least according to a bronze placard on its wall—and bound her hands and feet, the sun had set and a slight rain had started to fall; something I fully welcomed after so much time in the desert. As to whether the girl welcomed it also, who could say. For even though I set her near the opening (as well as the fire) and provided her my own bedroll to sit on, she only continued to glare—probably due to us eating in front of her; for I had decided, though you might think it cruel, that I would starve her into speaking, if necessary. Which, of course, she finally did—speak, that is—although only after a considerable time, saying, hoarsely, yet clearly, assertively, "Is this some kind of torture? I mean, don't you have to feed prisoners before killing them? Isn't that what the Geneva Convention says?"

I looked at her through the flames, saying nothing, even as Kesabe snarled.

At length I carved a piece of meat from the spit and dropped it on a paper plate, which I carried around to her—but didn't hand over. Instead, I knelt and sliced off a single bite-sized morsel—then held it close to her nose.

"Trade," I said, matter-of-factly. "One bite per something about you. It can be your name. Where you're from. How you've survived ... Just talk."

She started to protest but hesitated, searching my eyes, trying to judge intent. At last she said, "So what's with the war paint?"

I stood and began to walk away.

"Wait a minute—wait a minute—jeez, so we don't go there—fine. My name is ... it's Essie, all right? Essie McIntyre. I'm from Spokane."

I paused, looking over my shoulder. "Where?"

"Spokane. It—it's a city. In Washington."

"... D.C.?"

"State. Washington *State.*"

I returned and crouched near her again. "Okay. So ... how'd you get to be here?"

She didn't say anything—only opened her mouth wide.

"It–it's got an aftertaste ... just so you know." I fed her the piece of allosaur.

She chewed it up eagerly, voraciously–before pausing, making a face.

"It's the game," I said. "You have to get used to it."

"It's not that. It's just ..." She swallowed slowly, tentatively. "I had alligator once, in New Orleans–this, this reminds me of that. Only heavier, oilier. With an acrid aftertaste."

"That's the predator in it ... at least that's what they say." I cut her off another piece. "Would–would you like some more?"

"Yes, I think so, please. It's not terrible."

I fed her the piece from the end of my knife.

"What, what was the question?" She finished chewing and swallowed. "Oh, yes. How did I come to be here. Well, that's just it–" She paused suddenly and tilted her head. "Can I ask you something?"

I must have looked confused.

"Just one," she said, and tried to smile. "What is your name?"

There was a pregnant pause as I thought about it. It seemed only fair. "Satanta," I said, and cut her another piece. "Satanta–the Last."

"Satanta, the Last," she repeated, and shrugged. "Okay. Thanks. Guess I figured you weren't a

Brad." She opened her mouth wide, waiting for the next morsel, but relented when I shook my head. "Right. So—how I came to be here. Well, see, that's the conundrum, isn't it? Because the fact is—*I don't know."*

I squinted, unsure how to take that. "What do you mean?"

"Again, I'm sure I don't know. Only that ... I was at a stoplight—in Spokane—watching a stormfront roll in, when the news starting talking about, well, power outages, mostly, but also that people were going missing—I mean, not just one or two, say, over the course of weeks or even days, but, *dozens* of people, maybe hundreds, all at once, as though they'd never even existed. And I was just sort of wrapping my head around that, or trying to, when I noticed there were ... lights in the clouds. Shapes. Things that were above me at that point and seeming almost to ... to be looking down at me. To be targeting me. Me—on my little motor scooter—somewhere in the Spokane Valley." She laughed. "And the next thing I knew I was here," She indicated the Strip. "Scooter and all—just sort of dumped over on my side at Circus, Circus, and feeling ... almost as though I'd been tasked with something. As though there was something I was supposed to do. Though what it was I couldn't remember—and still can't, no matter how hard I try."

I'm afraid I just looked at her. What was there to say, exactly? That what she had described was impossible? That even though most the world's population had vanished and the dinosaurs had returned–an impossibility itself, but something we had accepted–her blacking out in one place and waking up in another was ridiculous?

"You should eat," I said, offering her more meat. "No more questions."

She pulled the flesh off the fork with her teeth and chewed, her eyes never leaving mine. "I have some," she said, talking around her food, "Questions, that is. Like, what the hell brought *you* here? And where do you get off on kidnapping me?"

I paused, knife in hand, as the fire crackled and popped.

"I–I came to sift ashes," I said–quietly, obliquely–but did not elaborate.

"You came ... to sift ashes," she said, and nodded once, twice. "Okay. I'll play. Why not. And these ashes are here, in Las Vegas?"

"In the suburbs, yes. On Canosa Avenue. It–it's all so foggy. I haven't been back for a very long time. But I'll know the way once I find the gas station."

"The gas station."

I nodded. "The one on the corner. The RGB. If it's still there."

"I see. And—and what do you plan to do with me?"

I looked at her in the firelight—at her auburn hair, which blazed in the fire's glow, and her green eyes, which caught the light and glimmered. "It is my wish that I should continue hearing your voice," I said.

She peered at me intensely, glimmeringly, as though she'd won some sort of victory. "Is that so?" Then she laughed, brusquely, boorishly, and held up her bound wrists. "Well, then. I guess you better start cutting, Chief. Wouldn't you say?"

"You're a real asshole, Satanta. Just so we're clear."

I turned around and looked up, shielding my eyes from the sun, and saw her glaring at me from Blucifer's saddle (to which I'd bound her with zip ties), before jerking the rein, tugging them after me.

"And here I thought you were different—if only for a minute," she continued. *"Boy,* was I wrong!"

"And I thought you were—how did you say it? On a speech strike," I said.

"I am," she snapped. "I just needed to say that one thing. Again."

We *clip-clopped* up S. Las Vegas Blvd, past the fairgrounds and a gaudy strip mall called the Bonanza, saying nothing, during which I found myself gazing at the sky lights–our ubiquitous friends since the Flashback–and noting how angry they seemed today, how inflamed; and noting, too, that Kesabe had not circled back in some time (for it was his tradition to run far ahead), a fact which was beginning to trouble me.

That's when I heard the strange sound: a kind of forlorn mewing, like the note of a horn being drug out too long, coming from just around the corner, just beyond the liquor store–and paused, holding up my hand.

"What? What's going on?"

I waved her into silence, dropping the rein, then hustled to the edge of the building–where, after peeking around the corner, I saw a juvenile sauropod of the Diplodocus family (meaning it was the size of a typical school bus) collapsed in the middle of the street–its right front leg stuck in a manhole.

"What is it? What do you see?"

I looked from the sauropod to the corner of a nearby building, where something had moved, then across the street to an overgrown alley. *Yes,* I thought. *There. And there. Between the tattoo parlor and the marijuana dispensary ...*

"Allosaurs," I said, gravely. "An entire pack of them. In desert camouflage. They–they've got something trapped."

"Omigod. It–it's not your dog, is it?"

I returned and picked up the rein, began leading Blucifer forward, into the intersection. "No."

"Wait ... what are you–"

"We're going through," I said.

"But what if those things–"

"They don't care about us; they want the bigger game. *For now.* Just hold on."

The horse's hooves went *clip-clop, clip-clop* as we passed, the bluish-gray sauropod coming into full view ...

A moment later she said, "It–it's stuck. In the manhole. Do you see that?"

I eyed the predators warily, continuing to lead. "There's nothing we can do about it."

"But she'll be helpless against–"

"That is the way of it," I insisted. "The way of the–"

"Look, would you stop with the Indian claptrap? I'm not even sure–"

There was a *thwomp* as the allosaur by the building leapt into the road–not by us but about fifty feet away, near the sauropod.

"Jesus, can't you do *anything?* What about your bow?"

"And risk bringing them down on us?" I intensified our pace, sprinting toward the Stratosphere. "No!"

And then they were coming–the allosaurs from across the street–passing so close we could smell the meat on their breath; closing in on the frightened herbivore ... until we passed the scene completely and sought refuge in a nearby gas station (its storefront had long since collapsed) and gathered there trembling as the sauropod cried out–for it wouldn't be long now until they fell upon her.

"Jesus," said Essie, listening. "What a world."

"Yes," I said, remembering. "My father used to say it had a demonic sublime; every tree and every rock, every animal, including man, down to the lowest insect." I listened as the sauropod moaned, seeming already to give up, to resign its fate. "And yet."

"What do you mean?"

"What?"

"You said, 'and yet.' What did you mean?"

I unshouldered the compound bow–rubbing my aching deltoid, stretching my arm. "Nothing. It's just that ... maybe it doesn't have to be this way."

When she didn't respond I looked at her–found her already looking at me: calmly, meditatively, her eyes seeming to glimmer. "I'm sure I don't know what you mean."

"I mean ... that I could end it. Her confusion and terror. That I–could prevent her from suffering." I looked at the bow and the dark, poisoned bolts attached to it. "That it's in my hands to do so."

"A mercy killing, then. Is that what you mean?"

"Yes," I said.

She seemed to think about it. "Well, you know, you'd have to expose yourself first—in order to take the shot. And there's always the risk they might turn on you. Is that—is that a risk you're willing to take? And if so ... why? How would it benefit you—or us?"

I stared at her, confused by the change. "Look, just a minute ago you were—"

"Just a minute ago I was participating," she said, sounding cold, analytical. "Now I'm observing. And I'll ask you again ... why? What could it possibly change?"

I gripped my bow and thought about that, wondering what had come over her, and why her eyes seemed to dance, to shine—as though they'd been illuminated from within.

At last I said, "Jesus. Maybe because we're still human?"

And then I was moving: stepping over the overgrown rubble, hurrying around the nearby buildings; dropping to one knee near the allosaurs where I sighted the mewing diplodocus and released two arrows, one after the other, into the soft tissue of her eye orbit, killing her instantly—after which the predators fell upon her like wolves, snarling and clawing, opening her like a bag of sausage, tearing out her throat ... as I walked back to the station and was greeted by Kesabe, barking and licking my hand. As I looked at Essie and found her returned to normal, seeming almost not to know what had happened.

As she indicated the orange Union 76 sign and said, in her usual tone of voice, "So would this happen to be it? Your gas station?"

After which I looked around in a daze—recognizing the soda fountain (now an antique) with the American bald eagle on top; recognizing the wooden Indian which stood by the door—and knowing, at last, that I had found my way home.

"It—it's not what I expected," said Essie over my shoulder, as Blucifer whinnied and Kesabe pissed on the nearest tree; as the overgrown rancher sat—its nearly flat roof baking in the sun ... its slat fence partially collapsed.

"It's not a teepee; if that's what you mean," I said, and dismounted.

"I didn't expect a *teepee,"* said Essie, as I helped her down. "It's just that—it's so *white.* Like Wally and the Beav are gonna come running out any minute."

"My father didn't believe in reservations," I said, leading Blucifer to a bush, abandoning the reins. "He thought they were museums full of defeated people; just so many relics, withering in the sun. He wouldn't even take us there to visit our grandparents; they had to come to us."

"That must have sucked."

"No, actually–it really didn't," I gripped the doorknob and paused, wondering if I was really up to it; if I was fully prepared for what I might find. "It taught us–my brother and I–to see ourselves as individuals, not a collective–and a defeated one at that. Maybe that's why neither of us wound up pickled in Thunderbird."

I twisted the knob and eased the door open, watching sunlight spill across the floor, then stepped in slowly, cautiously. "He didn't buy the idea that land could be any sort of birthright, said living things had always competed for resources and always would, and that, change being the only constant, to deny that was to deny the fundamental nature of reality."

I paused in front of a framed picture of my mother, touching it gently, tracing a finger through the dust. "He always said, 'Should I apologize for winning your mother from a white man?'"

I laughed a little, and so did Essie.

"'No, of course not,' he'd say. 'Because that's what nature does, it *conflicts.* It competes.'"

I stared at the picture, hoping it had been painless for them and that they had just vanished like so many others. Hoping they had gone together.

"Well, that explains that," said Essie. She had leaned in and was examining my face.

I must have looked confused.

"Your war paint," she said. "It's red and white."

And I had to laugh; because she was exactly right, even though I had never thought about it—had never even considered it, at least not consciously—after which, feeling cavalier, I said, "My real name is Steve, by the way. At least, that's what my mother used to call me."

She paused, looking at me with something like pity. "Steve."

"Yeah. It—it means victor—"

"I'm gonna stick with Satanta. If you don't mind."

"Sure," I said, and shrugged. "I prefer it. More apocalyptic."

And then we moved on, picking our way through the overgrown house (liberating a stack of photo albums along the way as well as my mother's Polaroid camera), after which we came to my old bedroom—the roof of which had collapsed so that the palm trees were visible outside—and sat on the bed.

"You had a beautiful life," said Essie at length—perusing the photos, turning the pages. "You were very lucky."

"I know," I said.

"Not everyone is."

"I know that, too."

I peeled the plastic coating from one of the sheets and removed a picture, staring at it in the late afternoon sun, in the burnt ocher wash of what photographers called the Golden Hour. "That was us—my entire family—at Disneyland; in Anaheim—must have been about '78 or '79. I can tell by the hair."

She leaned close to examine it, her own hair tickling my cheek. "Hard to believe that's you. *Mercy.* You had prettier locks than I did. So did your brother."

I rubbed the Polaroid between my thumb and forefinger, slowly, absently. "All dust," I said quietly. "Everything in the picture, both the red and the white." I laid back on the bed, feeling suddenly tired.

"Nonsense," she said—and, to my astonishment, laid down next me. "You seem alive enough to me."

And then she began to doze—or so it seemed to me—and it was just myself and the queer lights:

which glowed all of a color and showed nothing of their usual chaotic rhythms, but only looked down on us softly, ambiently, like Christmas lights hung from the very firmaments; serene.

If not for her having taken off her over-shirt during the night, we would never have found her—for it was only after giving it to Kesabe and having him sniff it that the Dutch Shepherd was able to track her: a trail which had led straight to the gas station and the allosaurs from the day before—not to mention Essie herself; who stood trembling yet defiant amongst the ruins and seemed almost to be goading the animals on, daring them to attack.

"Essie! Good God, Essie!" I shouted, fighting the reins, as Blucifer—panicked by the predators—leapt and circled and whinnied, kicking up dust. "What have you done?"

"Oh, don't you see? We had no right! No right at all!"

I dismounted quickly—having wrested Blucifer into submission only briefly, for he snorted and charged away even as I found my footing—unshouldering my bow as fast as I could, nocking a bolt. "Back up into the store, dammit; do it, now! *Why, for God's sake?"*

But she only held her ground—even as the sky strobed and flashed and the clouds roiled with thunder—her feet planted firmly; her arms held wide. "But don't you see it? *Oh, how can you not see it?* Look into my eyes, Satanta. Look into my eyes and tell me you don't understand ..."

I sighted the animal nearest her and released an arrow, *Thwish!* —which struck the beast in its eye and dropped it, instantly, even as Kesabe barked and snarled and the others seemed to zero in on me.

"Look at me, Satanta. Slay ... *me.* Because *they* are in me, now, fully manifest. They—who have caused all the suffering. They, the very architects of the Flashback. And I want them to *feel* it. Oh, can't you understand? I want them feel what it is they have wrought!"

I caught a fleeting glimpse of her before the remaining allosaurs attacked: saw the eyes like a fire in the sky and the sallow skin shot through with green—until the animals charged and I loosed another bolt, dropping one as it ran, and yet leaving two, both of which would have fallen on me if Kesabe hadn't leapt into the fray like a pointy-eared threshing machine, barking and biting, scratching and snarling, peeling the predator away, as the other bit for my neck and I dodged, leaping onto its back; then stabbed it with an arrow again and again, hanging on as it leapt and bucked, groping for its eyes (which I would have gouged out had it not fallen), thanking the Great Spirit as it shuddered and died.

And yet I'd barely had time to climb off it when I heard Essie scream—not from the store's rubble but high above it, in the sky—where a pterodactyl wheeled like a kite in the sun even while gripping her like a ragdoll and beaking her as if with a sword—that is until it too was attacked by another, bigger bird—at which I snatched up my bow and nocked my last arrow, aiming into the flail of talons and wings, and shot the first bird clean through its skull.

And then it was over, or nearly so, as the thing fluttered down and dropped her; at which I ran to her and cradled her in my arms even as the bird next to us thrashed and died.

"They felt it," she gasped, "I know they did. They felt it through me."

"Shhh," I said, "Save your strength. We have to get you—"

"They thought they could just see through my eyes—that they could observe us that way, study us ..." She coughed violently—shudderingly—hacking up blood. "But what they didn't know was that they'd *feel* through me too. Feel it all, Satanta ..." She groped for my hand and found it, began to squeeze. "The pain ... the terror. But also the compassion.

The mercy. Like the kind you showed the herbivore. The kind–" She seized up suddenly as though her insides were being torn apart. "The kind you showed me. That–that we showed each other. And for the briefest of moments ... they understood. Go–go north, okay? You'll find people there, good people. I know–because *they* know. Our watchers. Our destroyers. I have been in their minds. Go north. But first ... first help your ..."

And she died.

I closed her eyes. And that's when it hit me how quiet it was, and that I could no longer hear Kesabe barking–that indeed, I could no longer hear him at all.

My grandfather once said, in response to my father, "We all live on reservations, some of us just don't know it yet." And though I didn't understand that then, I was pretty sure–as I stood over my friends' graves and watched the house go up in flames–that I did now; for he'd been talking about our limitations and the fact of our own mortality (trying to tell me, I think, as I got ready to leave for Los Angeles more than 30 years ago, that if I were going there to escape I was in for a disappointment). All I know for certain is that as I stood there over the crude markers–one for Essie and one for Kesabe–I felt smaller and less significant than ever before (and I'd felt pretty small and insignificant since the Flashback), to the point that I questioned going on at all, north or otherwise. But then Blucifer showed up with a familiar snort and whinny—where he'd gone I didn't know, nor did I ask—after which, feeding him what remained of the oats in my pocket, I decided we would head back to the coast and follow it north, for maybe there *were* people there, 'good people,' as Essie had said, and if that were true, then, truly, anything was possible.

Even so I hesitated—even after mounting and slinging the bow across my back (for I hoped to find arrows before leaving the city entirely), thinking on Essie, whom I had come to love even though I'd known her only for a short time, and on my friend, Kesabe (whom I'd named 'Kemosabe' but had shortened to 'Kesabe') ... a dog who had just been a dog but thought he was a wolf; and who—as evidenced by his final act—sometimes was, sometimes was.

Like you, maybe? I wondered, and laughed. *Satanta the Last—come Steve?* And yet wasn't it at least partially true? For the Flashback made of you only what you already were—however veiled that may have been in the world before.

And then I snapped the reins and we went, Blucifer and I—back toward the coast and the passage north.

Back to the winding trail, which, like all winding trails, went everywhere and nowhere at once.

‘Dog’ is a Palindrome

In the movies they call it a “smash cut”–when the scene shifts so suddenly and abruptly that the viewer is knocked off balance, if only for an instant. That’s what it was like when Puck attacked the nanotyrannosaurs–which we hadn’t even known were there–smashing the silence into a thousand pieces as the animals burst into the clearing thrashing and gnashing their teeth and one of the predators broke off in pursuit of the man with the knife–the man who, only an instant before, had been holding the weapon to Lisa’s neck.

Not that I knew it was Puck yet. That wouldn’t come until after the mini-tyrannosaur had bitten off the man’s head and shoulders (and swallowed them whole) and returned to the fray; after which I snatched my pistol up from the ground and tried to find an opening–mortified that I might accidently shoot my own dog–and, finding it, squeezed the trigger.

Krack!

I fired twice more.

Krack! Krack!

And then the nanotyrannosaurs were down (but not before one of them had shaken Puck like a ragdoll and launched him into a nearby tree) and we were running toward him. Toward my dog who had gone missing during the Flashback and whom we had long since presumed dead. Toward the broken bundle of fur that had somehow found us and saved our lives.

"Puck!" I cried, trying to rouse him. "Come on, Boy. Wake up."

"Omigod. Omigod, Nick. Is he–?"

I crouched over him and felt his belly–which was bloated and distended, like that of a starving person–with my gloved hand.

"No. No–he's breathing. But shallow. Like he's in a coma." I looked around the clearing, at the dead tyrannosaurs and the dead man missing his head and shoulders, and at the *deadfall,* which was scattered everywhere, like rubbish. "It's going to take time. But look, there's firewood. And that brook can't be far–not at the rate we've been moving. I say we camp here."

Lisa fidgeted about nervously. "Here? How is that a good idea?"

"I don't know what else," I said. "We can't move him. He could have a broken neck, or internal bleeding–I mean, who knows. Besides, Nano-Ts are territorial. Which means the apex predators of this entire area are likely right here, just as dead as that man with the knife." I squinted at the animal that had killed him. "I hope it choked on it."

I was referring, of course, to my golden dog whistle, which the man had taken from me and put around his own neck when it became evident that we had nothing else of value.

"My God, Nick, but we're in the middle of nowhere. What if they hunt in packs and not pairs? That would mean there's still–"

"I'm not leaving him like this, okay?" I shot her a glance and she recoiled noticeably. Then, seeing how the harshness in my voice had disturbed her, I took a deep breath–and tried again. "Just, help me with the camp, okay? I can sit with him while you sleep. All right? I'll stay up and keep watch. If he doesn't wake by morning–I'll take care of it myself."

She looked at me as though she were about to cry. "I didn't say we should leave him, Nick. I– It's just that ..." Her eyes welled up suddenly and she batted away the tears. "Oh, fuck it all."

And she wandered off–to gather sticks for the fire, ostensibly, but really to avoid saying the only thing left to be said. Which was that in a world where the vanished outnumbered the living by something like 3 to 1–the "Big Empty," the old man at the filling station had called it–a world without civilization or creature comfort or compassion, which had regressed to the Stone Age and beyond—yea, even to primordia itself—in *that* world, what could it possibly matter?

I paused as the wind picked up and rattled the leaves. Well, what could it? What was it worth amongst so much human suffering, so much grief and loss? One animal's life. One mixed-breed dog.

I looked at Puck who lay motionless but breathing in the lengthening shadow of the tree.

Just a dog.

And then I did something I had sworn to never again do; something I had promised Lisa I would resist—did it knowing full well what consequence might come in a world populated by ghosts; by disappeared souls; by a few scattered survivors living every minute and every hour—every waking moment—in something like Hell.

I slipped off one of my gloves and laid a trembling hand on Puck's head.

After which, noting the itching sensation in my palms and fingertips, I let the golden eyes open—crustily, sleepily—one after the other, like blinking boils. And I began to *see.*

They'd appeared shortly before the Flashback—that strange system of storms which had caused so many millions to disappear and that had brought the terrible lizards; that cataclysm which had re-mapped Time itself—opening one by one over a period of weeks, itching and burning like white phosphorous. I suppose in time we would have sought medical help (although it is difficult to credit, even now, after witnessing the Flashback and its impossibilities firsthand, what could have resulted from that); but, as it turned out, Time was something we had not owned and never would—for it was owned exclusively by them: the masters of the lights in the sky. The architects of the storm.

None of which mattered during the Great Collapse, for by then we'd become like everyone else, struggling merely to survive, and the strange eyes—as inexplicable as they were—had, with the help of a pair of thick gloves, been almost forgotten. Nor, in truth, was this particularly difficult; the eyes, once covered, tended to close their lids and scab over.

All of which was just as well—because I hadn't been able to see through them anyway. At least, not until I touched the dying girl in Seattle—an incident I shall not speak of except to say, that—for a period of time—I saw all her yesterdays and all her hardships; all her life condensed up to that very moment, and more, I saw, for the briefest of instants, what had come *after*—which had been a thing of such raw beauty and terror it had nearly driven me mad. Indeed, I *would* have been mad had Lisa not been there to pull me away—nor, for that matter, had the ghosts of the Flashback—millions upon millions of them, pressing down on me from every corner and from every nook and cranny of the world—not driven me to distraction.

Suffice it to say that had been the last time—the last time I had allowed them any free reign: to see, to feel, to live vicariously through the lived experiences of others. After that, the gloves had stayed on. Stayed on as we trekked from Seattle through Tacoma and across the Olympic Peninsula to Aberdeen, where we had hoped to find Lisa's parents, but found only a house with a collapsed roof and a protoceratops nest in its kitchen. So, too, had we lost Puck, who had chased a turkey-like creature into the ruins of a T.J. Maxx in Olympia and never come out, even though a search revealed no other egress but the shattered front doors—which left us no choice but to assume he had vanished in some aftershock of the Flashback.

And now here we were, somewhere between Hoquiam and Ocean City, travelling through the forest instead of following the road because the road was rife with bandits and outliers (one of whom must have spied us through the trees before getting the jump on us shortly after the brook), and no closer to hope than we had been before—indeed, further from it than ever, and with three less bullets in the gun.

Worse, another would have to be used to put Puck down in the event he didn't wake up; something which seemed increasingly likely as the eyes in my hand perceived only a mottled fog and Lisa could be heard approaching us through the scrub.

"You're a fool, Nick Callahan. A fool. But I suppose you already knew that."

I allowed my hand to drop before plunking down in the fir needles and just staring into space. "There was nothing. I saw nothing. It–it was like he didn't even exist."

She sat down next to me and exhaled, tiredly.

"He's an animal–what did you expect?" She picked up my glove and offered it to me, but I didn't take it. "You said it yourself; it's like they see memories. The eyes. I don't imagine a dog has a particularly long one. Do you?"

I sighed. All I knew for certain was that I felt numb and more than a little tired. "I don't know. I don't know what I expected. Or what I was looking for. An incident, maybe. Some kind of clue."

She laid her head on my shoulder and stared at nothing, same as me. "What kind? A clue to what?"

"That's just it–I don't know. A clue to what might wake him up, I guess. Something I could say. Something that was important to him."

"His butt was important to him," she said. "A source of endless fascination."

I had to smile.

That's when it happened. That's when he yelped, ever so slightly, and his paw twitched.

I looked at Lisa and she looked back. And then my hand was on him and we were running—Puck and I—down cobblestone lanes lined with streetlamps and through pools of foggy light; through tides of rusted Maple leaves, which leapt and swirled as we passed.

"What is it?" I heard Lisa say, her voice growing smaller, more distant. "What do you see?"

I turned to look at Puck as we ran and saw his tongue loll and his eyes shift—as though he wanted to look behind himself—behind us—but didn't dare.

"Fear," I said. "Confusion." An image entered my mind of a dug passage beneath the rear wall of the T.J. Maxx; of the turkey-like thing crawling through it with Puck hot on its heels. "He escaped from beneath the wall and now he's lost somewhere in the fog. And he's terrified ... but of what I don't know. It's almost like—wait a minute. Wait a minute." I looked behind him—having heard something huffing and snorting—and saw a fully-grown therapod dinosaur (colored orange and black, like a Gila monster) bounding after us in the dark, gaining rapidly. "There's something coming—some kind of predator. An allosaur, I think. Whatever it is, it's closing, and I mean fast."

"Oh, my God. Nick. Can't you do anything? H-hello? Nick?"

"Lisa!"

But she was already gone, lost amidst the vision and the ghostly white noise of the dead; constrained to some other time and place—erased from my present condition completely.

Understand this. While there are several dog breeds known to climb trees—the New Guinea Singing Dog; the Louisiana Catahoula; the Treeing Walker Coonhound, and the Jack Russell Terrier (I know this because I have since read up on it), the Miniature American Shepherd, which is what Puck mostly resembled, is, most emphatically, *not* known for such behavior. So, you can imagine my fear and consternation when Puck veered for the nearest Maple tree and attacked it like it was a set of monkey bars—even as the allosaurus collided with it directly beneath him and proceeded to do the same, or tried to. Even now I'm in awe of the pluck and determination he showed that day—to seemingly defy gravity in such an impossible way and to dash up the tree's trunk like that, and then to hold onto the lowest branch in such an unshakable manner—it was truly a sight to behold. Especially when the allosaur began to leap and lunge and to snap at him and he briefly lost a paw-hold; before his hindlimbs kicked in and propelled him the rest of the way—into the tree's bowl and a relative amount of safety; into a position from which he could run along one of the branches onto the roof of the nearest house ... but didn't, as he needed to give the allosaur a piece of his mind.

Which he did, barking and yapping and snarling, even as I watched from below like Johnny Smith in *The Dead Zone*—I even had the collar of my peacoat turned up—standing next to the allosaur but in virtually no danger; inhabiting the scene while somehow remaining apart. Like a ghost.

That's when the other allosaurs showed up—at least one of them passing right through me—and began to triangulate the tree, at which Puck *did* run along one of the branches to the house—but hesitated before jumping from the eave; it was, after all, a long way down, even for a man. And that is where he remained—as the predators moved from the tree to the house and effectively surrounded it—after which there was little he could do but to sit on his haunches and try to wait them out.

Which, eventually, he did, although by this time the moon—which was visible through a part in the clouds—was directly overhead, and even I, a ghost, had the sense that several hours had passed. That's when he retraced his steps to the tree, and, after many false starts, skidded partially down its trunk before leaping the rest of the way to the ground.

"Good dog," I said, and attempted to pet him, "Smart dog ..."

But my hand just passed through him and he didn't notice me at all, just sniffed about the ground as he walked in tight circles and finally trotted away. Back up the lane toward the little strip mall and the T.J. Maxx; back through the gloom which was slowly starting to lift.

It was then that the scene changed and I was standing outside the store, standing where I had stood not 24 hours ago, blowing on that dog whistle; where I'd finally admitted to myself that he was either out of range or had been taken by the Flashback. Puck was there, just sitting on his haunches. I knelt in front of him and studied his face. Studied the patch of black fur around one eye and the eyes themselves, as deep and brown as any person's. Saw the doubt and desperation and the confusion and the *complexity.* And I saw something else, something I can only call, for lack of a better term, his humanity.

The wind gusted and trash skittered across the empty lot.

And yet there was something more–something deeper–wasn't there? Something just beyond my perception. And this was something–which was *not* human. A thing which, now that I've had time to understand it, was as pure and ephemeral as light itself.

In short, a thing utterly without guile or self. Perfect. Irreducible. Uncreated.

And then Puck barked, causing me to jump, and the moment was past, and I came out of it to the sound of a campfire crackling and Lisa shaking and cursing me awake, after which she said, with a clear tremor in her voice, "There's more of them out there. More Nano-Ts. *We have to go, Nick. Now."*

I looked at the corpses of the first Nano-Ts, which were being picked over by compies, the small but deadly predators which always accompanied a kill, then deeper into the dark, where I detected no movement. "How do you know? I don't hear anything ... just the compies."

"I did hear them," she said, and picked up a stick. "Two of them, at least, calling from different directions. They're triangulating us. We have to go, Nick. We have to go right now." She looked at Puck, her face half-painted in firelight. "I'm sorry."

I looked at him too—at the patch of black and his closed eyes, at his paws which had been bloodied by the tree's rough branches. "I—I can't. I'm sorry. Because ... there's something in there. Something I need to see. The eyes–Puck–there's something they want to show me. Something I need to understand."

I approached her suddenly and gripped her arm. "Something that might save us all–*but I need more time!"*

That's when we heard it–both of us–the unmistakable bark of a nanotyrannosaur, which was quickly answered by another, closer. Right at the tree line.

She cursed and jerked away. "Tell them!"

I looked at Puck and then back at her, then back to Puck ... when I noticed the revolver laying in the grass. "Ocean City–it's not that far." I rushed forward and snatched up the gun. "There's still two bullets. Take it."

She froze, looking at my extended arm, then into my eyes, which she searched. "You bastard ..." She welled up suddenly and intensely. "You *fucking bastard."*

I shook the gun. *"Goddammit, Lisa.* Take it."

She reached up slowly and took it.

"I will meet you in Ocean City. I'm ... I'm just going to try this one last time–okay? If it doesn't work ... I'll leave him. I promise."

"No–you won't." She smiled like a crazy person. "Because they're going to come in here and *rip you to shreds ..."*

"You don't know that. The fire will keep them away. The smell of their dead buddies ..."

She swiped at her cheeks and sniffed loudly. Then she moved toward the opposite tree line, the one facing the road–and paused. She turned around. "You're a fool, Nick Callahan. A fool. But I suppose you already know that."

"Get out of here," I said.

And she went.

I rushed over to Puck and dropped to my knees.

"Okay, buddy. You need to show me what you got, and show me fast, all right?" I placed my hand on his head and squeezed slightly. "You remember Dad. He used to take you fishing–like, every Sunday. Remember that? Well, he used to say that to understand a man you had to walk a mile in his shoes. That, to open a man's heart, you had to know something about his journey; about what made him tick. So ... I'm walking in your shoes. I'm walking in them right now. And what I need to know is ... what will wake you up, okay? I need you to show me. Show me, Puck. Be a good dog one last time. Come on, buddy. Let it go."

And then I closed my lids and let my hand take over–let the golden eyes re-open and peer through Time itself. Let them read Puck's yesterday as the compies chittered and the Nano-Ts barked, coordinating their attack; as Lisa made her way to

Ocean City and the lost souls of the Flashback began to cry and howl their laments.

The trail had gone cold. I could see it in his eyes as he trotted to a halt at the edge of Highway 109 and sniffed at the air, his white coat blowing.

Come on, boy, I thought, beginning to worry. I was standing by a green and white road sign which read: OCEAN CITY–22 MILES. *You can do it. Don't give up on us.*

He sat on his haunches and looked around, panting. At the abandoned motor home Lisa and I had dozed in only a few hours before; at the cracked and potholed highway which had been overrun with prehistoric lichen.

Come on, buddy. Go sniff up that RV–it'll put you back on the trail. Just get up and get moving. Because that man with the knife is probably watching us–Lisa and I–right now. So are the Nano-Ts, like they are in the present. And we're never going to make it without you.

Then, like a miracle, he was up again–his tail wagging furiously, his ears twitching puckishly–investigating the Coachman, tearing off toward Ocean City. Barking and yelping, which rode the wind like an echo.

I opened my eyes—*my eyes,* not the alien things in my hands—and saw the branches shaking deep in the dark. They were on the move again—the Nano-Ts—closer even than before. They were getting ready to strike; to do what they did best, which was to rend and kill. I shut my lids and refocused, feeling as though Time had fast forwarded, as though it had leapt ahead.

Show me, I thought. *Show me now, or forever hold your peace. Show me or see us all join the choir of the damned!*

And that's when it happened: that's when I saw it, the moment that had changed—still would change—everything. That moment Puck had skidded to a stop after surpassing our location and begun to cock his head, and to tilt it quizzically; to look from the road to the tree line and sniff at the briny air—to bolt into the woods like a maniac and, apprehending the situation quickly and accurately, to attack the Nano-Ts.

For that was the moment the man with the knife had tested the dog whistle. The instant in which he had placed it to his lips and blown once, hard and long, and that he had grinned his rotten-toothed grin and said, "Now kick that gun over here, nice and easy. Come on, now. Nobody wants to see Missy here all cut up like Sharon Tate."

Indeed, it was the moment that had led to our rescue and to Puck being in a coma; and to him being in limbo, like the victims of the Flashback and its great and terrible Vanishing, trapped in Time, caught between worlds. A place I knew I could never have left him, not if it had cost me everything I had.

Which it may have, I thought, as I came up out of the trance and looked at the dead beast that had killed the knifeman—for I knew what I had to do—and also through the firs, beyond which Lisa had disappeared. *It may have.*

Then I was up; I was on my feet—snatching the man's knife from the forest floor, falling on the carcass like a jackal—scattering the compies in a flurry.

Drawing the blade across its belly so that its innards exploded out like writhing red snakes.

"Hold on, Puck," I shouted, as I waded into its guts. "You're going to like this! Going to jump right to attention, I guarantee it ..."

I slashed and slashed—clearing away the bowels, cutting away viscera—even as the compies returned, leaping and scurrying. "Hold on, buddy! We got this—"

And they descended on me, or rather ascended me, scurrying up my legs and back, piling up on my shoulders, attacking my face as I located the stomach and cut it open and began feeling around. *"Ahh–ahhh ...!"*

I collapsed amidst the guts and gruel, batting at my face, at their little beaks and talons, even as the firs shook and I realized I could *smell* them–the Nano-Ts–hovering in the black between trees, getting ready to pounce.

I pulled one of the compies off and wrung its neck before climbing back up and reaching into the T's stomach again, after which I felt something unusual, something round and smooth, and withdrew it quickly–only to realize it was one of the knifeman's eyeballs.

"Jesus!" I cursed, and dropped it–even as the compies swarmed over me like mutated sewer rats, like blood-sucking bats, causing me to fall into the viscera again and to roll up like a fetus, to cry out in anguish–knowing, at last, that it was truly over; that there would be no escape for us this time, neither Puck or I, and wondering what Lisa would do now that she was all by herself–and how she would survive–wondering if she would always hate me for the decisions I'd made and for my bullheadedness, and for a thousand other–

"Goddamnit, Nick, find the fucking whistle–I got this!"

I swiped the blood from my eyes and looked at her–saw her stomping and stabbing compies as though she were a mad woman, as though she were fighting in the trenches of France. She knew. She had figured it out herself. Woman's intuition, perhaps, who knew?

And then I was up and reaching into the thing's stomach, desperately feeling around, praying that the stuff that felt like macaroni and cheese wasn't the knifeman's brains—and yet knowing it was—finding the golden whistle suddenly and unexpectedly and placing it in my mouth.

Where I blew on it as hard as I could, sending a frequency only Puck could hear pulsating through the air.

After which, like gray ghosts, the Nano-Ts began to emerge—slowly, cautiously, not pouncing suddenly as I'd expected, but surrounding us in a loose but ever-tightening circle. Corralling us.

"I'm sorry," I said, as the Alpha bull approached the corpses one at a time and sniffed them carefully, thoroughly. "You should have gone to Ocean City."

She looked at me in the dark, the fire having long gone out. "And live ... I suppose," she said. She smiled wanly. "For what?"

And then something moved and we turned to look at it, and it was Puck, standing on all fours and just as awake as could be.

Puck. Who growled at the dinosaurs threateningly even as he crept forward like a puma and finally paused between us—facing off with the bear-sized predators resolutely, glowering at them without fear or hesitation.

The wind blew, and the trees swayed. The Alpha bull sniffed at the air. My heart thudded in my chest even as it looked at the corpses and then back to Puck. Then it did it again.

And then it swung its great head away and turned, its massive bulk pivoting smoothly, gracefully, and glided back into the trees, after which the others began to peel away and follow—until they were gone, all of them, and we were alone.

Just us and Puck, who was still covered in the predators' blood. Just us and a shepherd mutt—ostensibly an American Miniature—who had been on one helluva journey, but was home now.

A mutt who licked our faces as we surrounded him and looked at us with such seasoned calm and selflessness that I was both spellbound and awed, as though I were in the presence of something at once human and more than human—something which was the epitome of love and faithfulness—something perfect, something divine. Something which came up the same thing no matter which way you turned it.

"Dog" is a palindrome.

The Elephant Slayer

It was called Netherville, which wasn't too bad a name compared to some of the settlements I'd been to: places like Misery, Montana and Malaise, North Dakota; Grimburg, Texas; Forsaken Falls, Idaho. I guess you could say that American towns have always had ominous names—that it was part of our frontier heritage—but then, I wasn't in America anymore, I was in Canada. Edmonton, Alberta to be precise. The Big E, as they called it.

As for how I'd come to be there—I'd rather not talk about it, and it's not important, anyway. Suffice it to say I'd caught a broadcast on the radio of my new Cadillac Escalade (Thanks, Butte Auto Sales, I left a silver dollar in the break room) which had urged me to go north to a town called Paradise—a town I'd mistaken for Paradise, Alberta, and so overshot by about 500 miles. Luckily for me, I'd come to Netherville before running out of gas (the Escalade's tank had been completely full, go figure; that's why I'd chosen it) and found a friendly settlement in spite of my folly.

At least, it had been friendly so far. In my experience, these things could–and often did–change on a dime. Which is about what I had on me when I walked into the 'Goodbye to All That' Saloon and ordered a drink at the makeshift bar; a bar whose counter had been fashioned from the scorched wing of an airplane.

"Keep it," said the bartender, a largish man with thick stubble and bad teeth, as he pushed back the coins. "First visit's on us, always."

He moved toward the back door–which was propped open with a rifle; probably due to heat from the firepit–walking awkwardly, haltingly, as though he had a bad hip. "Beer's out back–in the snow."

I glanced around the room as he went: at the other patrons–bearded men, all of them–who had peeled off coats and hats; and at one who hadn't–a lone figure sitting in the corner ... with a pair of crutches nearby.

"That includes the mastodon; the mammoth. The roast elephant, whatever you want to call it."

He shuffled back, slowly, arduously, twisting the cap off a bottle of Molson, setting it down. "It's good–fresh. The meat, eh, not the beer. It was harvested only yesterday."

He laughed a little and shook his head. "Whatever he does with that ivory, I'll never know."

I looked at the bottle of beer, which had foamed over onto the counter–onto the Cessna's battered wing. "What who does with it?"

"What?"

"What *who* does with the ivory?"

He lifted the bottle and wiped around the rivets, fussily, fastidiously. "Oh, yuh. You're the new guy. Why, Gavin Carter, of course. Our mysterious and storied *Great White Hunter.*"

"Our Nanook of the North!" hollered a nearby patron, lifting his sloshing glass. "The Elephant Slayer of Alberta."

"Or at least the frozen shithole that used to be Alberta," said another.

I must have looked confused.

"Local hero," explained the bartender. "Big-time trophy hunter. Lives in that house up on the ridge; the one with the orange roof–the old Riblet Mansion. Just helped himself to it one day. But he's a hero because he hunts the mammoth–and I mean consistently, successfully–and keeps the town fed."

A patron leaned in abruptly, thoughtlessly–as drunk people are wont to do–his breath reeking of Molson. "Speakin' a which–I'll take some more of that, eh? The stew."

"Well, that depends, Liam," said the bartender. "Where is your bowl?"

The man looked around, dazed and confused, until his glassy eyes settled on the back of the room—and the booth next to the solitary figure.

"Never mind, Liam," said the bartender warily. "I'll get it for you. Just relax." He gave me a little bow. "Excuse me."

"Of course," I said.

And then I took my first drink and paused—savoring it. Savoring its bite and its body and its bitterness and its perfection. Worshiping it; and focusing upon it to the exclusion of all else. Because the truth of it was, drinking it was like drinking civilization itself.

The drunk, meanwhile, was just staring at me: as though he knew me, perhaps, or maybe not. As though he loved me, perhaps—but maybe hated me too. As though there was something on his mind that he just had to say—if he could just untangle his thoughts and find the right words. If he could just get his mouth to open and his tongue to—

"Don't," I said.

And he didn't—talk to me, that is—after which the bartender returned and fetched me another beer—saying, as he twisted the cap off and set it down, "Compliments of the young lady in the corner."

I looked over my shoulder and saw that the figure had unzipped its coat and removed its scarf and hat—revealing a woman with black, unkempt hair and harsh, asymmetrical features (and yet attractive, for all that) who couldn't have been more than, say, twenty-five. A woman who looked at me with such startling clarity and matter-of-factness that I almost averted my eyes—but didn't, because I didn't want to appear weak. Instead, I just smiled—confidently, breezily (at least that was my schtick), raising my beer bottle. As though I wasn't just Travis Hayes, UPS delivery driver from Denver, Colorado, but Travis-*fucking*-Hayes, Carefree Stud of the Apocalypse.

That's when it happened; when the fight broke out, erupting in a flurry of broken glass and expletives (and flying booze), toppling the nearby barstools.

"Hey, goddamnit!" shouted the bartender, as I scrambled clear of the melee—which, surprise! involved the man who had been staring at me—"Hey, hey, hey!"

And then everything was noise and fury as others joined in and I turned to check on the black-haired girl (although *why* I am not certain; she could clearly take care of herself), but saw only an empty booth. Everything was chaos and confusion as I stared into her corner and noted the missing crutches—but couldn't for the life of me figure out where they—or she—had gone.

I looked to where a wooden door swung back and forth in the wind, letting in gusts of snow. The side alley, of course—!

And then I was moving—double-timing it, as we used to say in the corps—dodging a pair of brawlers, bursting into the alley; pausing by a heap of garbage as I noticed there were no footprints in the snow and thus no way to—

At which my vision winked out and I could see only stars, like scratches in space-time itself. At which I saw only comets—which darted and swirled, ember-like, as I fell.

"Ah, ah! Here he comes. You see now, Eska? You didn't hit him so hard after all. Our sleeper has awakened."

I blinked, clearing my eyes, as the room swam into focus: as the floating spheres of light resolved into candle flames and the hovering pink blur became a face, which smiled—patiently, fatherly. Elusively, like a wolf.

"Welcome to the Roc's Nest," said the face—its skin cracked like bleached leather, its teeth straight and white. "Please, have a look around. I'm Gavin Carter. And this—this here is Eska. My adopted daughter."

I looked at her even as I became aware of my pounding head: at her strange, harsh face and dense, un-manicured brows; her large, stout teeth—which were *not* straight and white—her eyes like chiseled obsidian.

"Go on, Eska," said the man—Carter—who appeared to be in his late 50s. "Be a dear and give Mr. Hayes a smile. Show him some of that primal charm you have; and in such great abundance. Come, come, now."

I watched as the corners of her mouth crept up, slowly, hesitantly. Indeed, she *could* be charming—even beautiful—when she wasn't braining you with a board, that is (or whatever she'd used).

I looked around the room, which was more like a great hall—at the pillars made of immense tree trunks and crossbeams carved from maple or walnut; at the astounding collection of mounted animal busts which adorned every wall and flat surface.

At last I managed, "How—how do you know my name?"

"It wasn't difficult," he said, taking a sip from his wine glass, dabbing at the corners of his mouth. "You still had an I.D."

I slapped my back pocket—my ankle catching on something as I shifted—but it was gone, of course. My wallet. That's when I looked down—having heard the *ka-chink* of metal—and realized I was shackled to my chair.

He frowned almost sheepishly. "An imposition, to be sure—but a necessary one." He looked at something on the table which I recognized as my old military ID. "Can't have a trained killer just wandering about the house—now can we?" He paused, studying my face. "I must say ... you don't exactly look the part."

"Well, people can be full of surprises, can't they?" I glanced at Eska, who just stared right back. "Your 'daughter' is certainly capable of a few. Wouldn't you say?"

"Oh, most certainly," said Carter—and added: "People, I mean. *People* are full of surprises. Not Eska. Not from me."

I raised an eyebrow.

"I know her too well ... having reared her since she was a pup." He paused, appearing wistful—even morose—before changing the subject; abruptly, I thought. "I, ah, couldn't help but to notice you appreciating my collection. Do you hunt, Mr. Hayes?"

I looked at the nearest mount, a triceratops head with a broken horn (and a frightful visage), wondering what the circumstances of its death had been. Had it been charging—with the Flashback in its eyes, perhaps—and thus *aware* that it had an opponent? Or had it been unaware, just mulling its soft grasses, until the bullet entered its brain?

"No," I said, finally, turning my attention back to him. "Can't exactly say as I am. It–it's never seemed like a fair contest to me." I jerked my leg against the chain–twice–to make a point. "Does it to you?"

"Pshaw," he protested. "You speak as if we're enemies. As though this were some contest between you and I, personally. On the contrary, Mr. Hayes. *It's a collaboration."*

I'm afraid I just stared at him.

At last I said: "Okay–why not. I'll bite. What are you talking about?"

"I am talking, Mr. Hayes ..." He stood and began pacing the length of the table. "–about *legend.* About myth and memory–and the securing of one's place in the natural order of things." He withdrew something from his housecoat as he walked–a pipe; but didn't light it. *"Posterity* is what I'm talking about. A place at the table of the gods. That, and endings. Inevitabilities."

He paused and struck a match. "One last and penultimate hunt."

He lit the pipe and waved out the match, then turned, slowly, regarding me through a cloud of smoke. *"Atatilla,* is what I'm talking about. Queen of the Mammoths. The, ah, Leviathan of the Steppes, as they say. I intend to kill her. And you, my lost and wayward friend, are going to help me. By acting as my driver."

"Your *driver?*"

"Yes. I'd normally call on Eska, but, as you've no doubt observed, she is—at present—incapacitated." He glanced at her across the table. "Isn't that right, Love?"

She took her eyes off me long enough to nod at him, stoically, silently.

"She, ah, understands, you see." He moved around the table toward her. "And not only the language but, how shall I say it? The lay of the land."

I watched as he took up position behind her and placed his hands on her shoulders.

At length I said: "What is it, Carter? And what is she? Cro-Magnon? Neanderthal? What do you mean— 'the lay of the land?'"

"I mean, she understands who she is ... now. And also, where she belongs." He fussed over her as she stared straight ahead—straightening her collar, repositioning her hair. "More importantly, she understands who *I* am. She can even say it—can't you, Love?"

She looked up at him with what seemed like respect, even reverence.

"Go on," he cajoled—gently. Softly. "Who am I?"

“Ma–ma–master,” she managed at some length. “You are ... Master.”

He veritably leapt with joy. “Very good, Eska! Oh, very good! Oh, that is absolutely wonderful. Most excellent. Now tell me, what I am the master *of?”*

She hesitated–as though searching her memory.

“E-everything,” she said at last, the words seeming to come easier, if not any faster. “M-m-me. The animals. All–all the world.”

“Yes, yes,” he said, and practically capered. “Very good ...”

He looked at me as though he assumed I’d be impressed. “Well? What do you think? Does she pass the test for *Homo sapiens sapiens?”*

But by then my anger had boiled over and I’d stood, abruptly, jerking the chain on my ankle as I moved toward him, dragging the chair after me.

“Look–you indoctrinate all the *Cro-Magnon fucking girls* you want ... If you don’t have me out of here inside of *60 seconds* I’m going to–”

“Genghis!” he shouted, and snapped his fingers, the sound of which echoed in the hall. “Come along, now. *Right now.”*

And before I could do much of anything he–*it*–was there, entering the room from a nearby corridor and snarling as it advanced, crouching and tensing as its foreclaws splayed; tapping its retractable sickle claws over the smooth, polished floor.

Stalking me as I fell, tangled up with the chair; and blanketing me with its shadow—as only a Utahraptor could.

"Freeze!" barked Carter—and the mottled orange and black Utahraptor froze, its knife-shaped head only inches from my own, its breath smelling of fish and rotted meat. "Hold."

And the Utahraptor held: snarling and growling—hissing, even, like a snake.

"There, see? There's nothing to be afraid of," said Carter, calmly. "Now, if we can avoid any further outbursts—let's continue, shall we? Where was I ..."

"Call it off," I said, shrinking away from the thing's muzzle, staring at its yellowed teeth (between which I could see bits of decaying flesh). *"Call it off, Carter."*

"Ah—well. So much for the vaunted bravery of the U.S. Armed Forces, eh?" He snapped his fingers quickly, crisply. "Kennel." But the Utahraptor didn't budge—indeed, I was pretty sure it only moved closer. "Genghis!" he barked. "I said, 'Kennel!' *Now!"*

At which the predator *did* move, although grudgingly, defying its master to the extent that it circled me quickly before breaking off and vanishing the way it had come, its tail whipping after it.

"There, you see? I can be reasonable." He paused as though he were looking at me. "Good heavens, Mr. Hayes! You look as though you've seen a ghost."

I pulled myself together as my breath came and went in ragged gasps. "What was that? Your hunting dog?"

"If you like." He paced over to the far wall–which wasn't, in fact, even a wall, but a towering black curtain–and stood to one side of it. "I want to show you something." To Eska he said: "Leave us. Tend to Genghis."

And she was gone.

He drew open the curtains.

"Behold, if you will, the Terror of the North–Ursus Maritimus Tyrannus, otherwise known as the Pleistocene Polar Bear."

My jaw dropped a little as the massive thing came into view–mounted not in a pose but as an enormous rug, which had been affixed to the wall, itself painted black.

"Magnificent–isn't she? 'There 'mid grand icebergs slipping *from* the cliffs, or on the drifting floes that choked the tide ... gigantic Polar bears, so grim and gaunt ... in solitary majesty abide.'" He turned to face me in the semi-darkness. "Isaac McLellan."

"Look, Carter. Would you just get to the–"

"But she wasn't solitary, Mr. Hayes–not this one. Nor did she have a sleuth of cubs. And yet she was–indisputably–a mother. No, what she had, my wayward friend, was *a* cub. A cub who was but an infant then but has since matured–at an accelerated rate, of course–into adulthood."

My eyes must have grown large as awareness dawned. "Eska. You're talking about Eska. But how could–I mean, the Flashback only happened less than–"

"Come now." He looked at me with something like pity. "Surely you've encountered it; that aberration in the Flashback by which a person–seemingly at random–begins to age–rapidly, I mean, exponentially–out of all context with their surroundings? Well, that's what happened to Eska. As for the hows and whys: such as why that process halted at her current state, or how she came to be living with prehistoric bears in the first place–who can say?"

I stared at the massive hide, at the flattened body and carefully preserved claws, and at the great head, which was big as a T. rex's. "How much does she know?"

"As with everything, only what I have taught her, of course. That I found her mother already slaughtered—by a cold-weather predator mightier even than she." He drew the curtains and walked toward me. "A story that was true—if not entirely factual."

I got up slowly, shaking my head. "And that was you ... The Great White Hunter of the Wastes. How ironic."

"Ironic, Mr. Hayes?" He paused and lifted his chin. "How so?"

"Because you seem so prissy and effeminate. I guess it's just hard to—"

And I lunged at him—chair and Genghis be damned—before something struck me in the head (a fire poker, as it turned out; wielded by Eska herself) and rendered me unconscious, if only for an instant.

"Really, Mr. Hayes," he said, circling me where I lay. "These outbursts will be your undoing. Irregardless, there you have it. Everything you need to know in order to help us with our hunt. You've even seen the bar we must surpass—the gold standard, as they say; the mount stuffed by Fidelio himself—my taxidermist, God rest his soul—before he showed Genghis an affection at the wrong time and place, and when the animal was in the wrong mood."

He removed a coin-like medallion from beneath his shirt and studied it, wistfully. "Dear Fidelio, who fashioned this."

He leaned close to show it to me and I saw a gold disk with an engraved bear on it—Ursus Maritimus Tyrannus. The Terror of the North. Eska's adoptive mother. "A reminder of my greatest prize to date."

He turned toward Eska. "Thank you, by the way. Although I must caution you; do not enter the room without my permission again, eh?"

I looked back and forth between them.

"Y-yes, Master," she struggled to say. "Eska is s-sorry."

He looked down at me. "Well, there, see? She learns. No need for another confrontation at the top of the stairs ... isn't that right, Eska?"

I looked at the splint on her ankle and the single crutch she was using.

At last I said, "I'll help you with your hunt, Carter. We—we'll kill this ... Atatilla. From the truck, isn't that right? Like cowards. But I'm going to kill you too, you bastard. Somehow, someway. You just watch."

Again, he looked at me with pity—or something like it. "I'm sure you'll try." And then he shouted down the hall: "Genghis, my boy! Snap to, old friend! It's time to release the hounds and hunt again!"

I guess I don't know what I expected when Genghis—having paused outside the vehicle's windows to sniff at the crisp air—leapt forward suddenly and vanished into the gloom. I suppose I was expecting the same result as the last twenty times he'd done this; which was nothing (although he had, at one point, emerged with a dead possum in his mouth). What I was *not* expecting was the wooly mountain that emerged—with Genghis clinging to its back—a thing easily the size of an industrial dump truck; which thundered past us on our left even as Eska pressed the knife to my throat and Carter readied his rifle—indeed, even as I put the Jeep into gear and prayed, having already been nicked once, that I wouldn't displease her, the fucking driving critic, again.

"Very well, Mr. Hayes—that's it," said Carter, aiming his rifle—a .460 caliber Weatherby Mark V he'd been droning on about since we left—squinting into its scope. "Now draw alongside—that's right. Step on the gas."

I stepped on the gas, disturbed by the lack of visibility—the lack of *road*—terrified we might plummet into a ditch (or even a chasm), *knowing* I had to do something–anything–to stop the madness.

"Faster, Mr. Hayes," he persisted, as the Jeep bounced and jolted and he struggled to maintain his aim. "Faster, damn you! Align us with her head. *Quickly,* or we'll lose them both."

I went faster–the great mammoth thundering along beside us as Genghis tore at her flank and the snow continued to fly; as Eska held the knife to my throat; and, due to the truck's jouncing, nicked me again and again.

At last I shouted: "You don't have to do this, Eska–all right? Can you understand that? You don't have to do what he says. *Nobody does.* Listen to me."

I stared at her through the rearview mirror: at her strange, dark eyes and sharply-chiseled features; at her tangles of black hair and large, uneven teeth, until she diverted her attention back to Carter, who was focused, exclusively now, on the stampeding elephant–and appeared almost to ask his permission.

"Ah, don't worry about him," I said, re-concentrating on my driving. "Can't you see he's busy?" I glanced at Carter–who ground his rifle scope silently, intensely. "He's too focused on that pachyderm." I jerked the wheel once so that the

Jeep rocked violently and he lost his target. "Isn't that right, Carter?"

"Eska!" he snapped.

I stiffened as her blade—having relaxed briefly—re-pressed against my throat; only harder, sharper, drawing new blood, then nodded, quickly, indicating the mammoth.

"Look at it, Eska," I said, having to raise my voice over the sound of its trumpeting, "Look at *her.* Look at how mighty and beautiful she is—how unspoiled and magnificent. What does she remind you of—Eska of the Great White Bears, of the animals who found you when you were lost and without hope; when you needed food and shelter and compassion—what does she remind you of and who in all the world could kill such a unique and powerful beast?"

I glanced at her in the mirror even as a shot rang out and she jumped—her dark eyes looking at Carter as he worked the bolt and ejected the casing; her focus shifting to the elephant at it cried out thunderously and increased its speed.

"Who, indeed, Eska," I said. "But the *Master of All?"*

She looked at me through the mirror and we locked eyes immediately—even as I continued to drive, blindly, recklessly.

"Yes, Eska. *M-M-Master.* The master of you—and of all living things. Who but he could have—or would have—killed your mother?"

I reached out suddenly and yanked the medallion from around Carter's neck.

"Your mother, Eska," I said, shaking the engraving—forcing her to look at it. *"This, right here!"*

And she took it; even as I faced forward briefly and began to slow down, and the giants, still at war, quickly pulled ahead—vanishing at last into the snow-speckled gloom.

Carter was enraged, incensed, speechless.

"What—what is the meaning of this?" He gripped his rifle, trembling with anger, then looked from me to Eska, his face swollen and red. "What have you ..." He exploded suddenly, violently, pathologically. "What have you *done, you animal?"*

I watched her in the silence.

"M-mother," she managed, staring at the gold coin, processing, it seemed, in the still, dark vehicle. "M-master*."* She looked at me as though struggling up from dream—and finally back to Carter. "Master ... *kill* ... Mother."

Carter shook his head, desperately, I thought, even fearfully. *"Pshaw!* This is nonsense! Killed your mother! What *rubbish.* Come here, child. Let me–"

And then the knife entered his throat and he gasped–gasped and choked and gargled–as the blood bubbled up and he wretched on it; as Eska twisted the blade.

He opened his door and fell to the ground, dropping his rifle which discharged–the sound of it echoing along the hills–prompting me to get out as well.

"Hold on, man!" I shouted, slipping and sliding around the hood, unzipping and yanking off my coat–crouching over him as he rolled in his own piss and blood. "We'll tie the sleeves together; make a tourniquet ..."

But he only got up and staggered further away: holding his throat, hemorrhaging into the clean, white snow, crying out as he slipped and fell and struck his head ... even as the ground shook with mighty footfalls, with the approach of something like a god.

That's when she emerged, the mastodon–*Atatilla* herself, having defeated Genghis–and lumbered to within a few feet of us, her shadow falling over us like a shroud.

"Easy ... easy," I said, stepping back slowly, gazing up at her face (which seemed positively ancient, positively eldritch). "It's all over now. It's—everything's done. You've won, old girl. You've survived."

The wind blew and the snow fell, clinging to her trunk and the folds of her face, sticking to her eyes, like cotton lint.

"I—I ..." Carter managed, the blood bubbling up like Karo syrup, like thick, black ichor, congealing on his chin and at the corners of his mouth, pulsing from his throat like little bursts from a squirt gun. "I ... am your master," he wheezed at last, and stared up at the thing in defiance, in cold-stone obstinance, smiling red, smiling like a lunatic, which I suppose he was, refusing to concede—to give even a centimeter.

And then she lifted her great foot and brought it down, missing me by just a few scant feet, and smashed Carter flat—raising it a couple seconds later to reveal a body thin as a bear rug but with its head and limbs intact. Leaving him like a trophy, like a warning to all who would challenge her, before lumbering back into the gloom and receding like a ghost, a legend—Atatilla, Slayer of Carter—master to all she surveyed.

You might say we made a strange couple, Eska and I. It's certainly possible, considering the odd looks we garnered on our return to Netherville.

Whatever the case, I saw no reason to part now that we'd established a means of communication (Carter had begun to teach her American Sign Language, which I was familiar with from my days as an interpreter). More to the point, I could never have simply abandoned her; not to the snowy wastes, and not to Carter's empty mausoleum (whose fuel stores for the generators were nearly depleted anyway).

And so we just went, stopping in Netherville only long enough to refuel the Jeep and to stock up on supplies, before beginning the long drive to Paradise, Montana, and also, more specifically, a place called Barley's Hot Springs.

For we had caught the broadcast again (the same one I had heard earlier) on our way in from the wastes. A broadcast calling itself Radio Free Montana—which had promised, among other things, a climate utterly unlike other settlements, and that, and I quote: "Here, indeed, is where civilization begins!"

It seemed worth another try.

As for this document and my need to put it to paper—and deliver it to the town repository—who knows? Maybe I just wanted to make sure history was recorded right. God knows, it rarely is.

And finally, for whoever may find this and wonder at its context—in a future, perhaps, where that context has become mere dust and memory—I offer this:

Welcome to the Big Empty, the world after the Flashback, a world in which most the population has vanished and where dinosaurs roam freely. You can survive here, if you're lucky, and if you're not in the wrong place at the wrong time, which is everywhere and all the time. But what you'll never do is remain the same, for this a world whose very purpose, it seems, is to change you, for better or for worse.

I recall watching Eska study the engraving on the way in, her face full of sorrow and yet complexity too, realizing, even then, that I need never fear her again, in light of which, I'll add:

It is my most fervent hope that it change you for the better.

The Devil's Triangle

Because our days were so exhausting, I was usually out the instant I hit the pillow, entering a deep and perfect sleep the dreams of which I could not recall; on other days, the work continued—the only difference being that in the dreams I flew over the island like a hawk (rather than search it house by house, or, just as often, beach café by tiki bar); and was able to spot a bread crumb even while soaring high enough to see most of Alice Town (though not so far as Bailey Town). And always, always, I returned to the Bimini Big Game Resort and Marina, with its ruined, capsized boats and broken, shattered docks (now undulating against the seawall); its multiple floors and long, red roof—which, only weeks before, had been the only thing standing between Búi and I (and Amanda, too) and the tsunami. Nor did I merely revisit it in my dreams, for it was where I started and ended each day's search regardless of how much of the island we'd cleared (we'd reached Resorts World Bimini—the approximate halfway point between Alice Town and Bailey Town). It was where I was at, looking at Búi's many half-filled water glasses, when I heard Amanda's voice crackle suddenly, startlingly, over the walkie: "Sebastian, I'm a few houses past Resorts World—on the state-side of the key. And, ah, you're going to want to see this." She quickly added: "It's not a body, nothing like that. It's nothing to do with Búi. Just—get over here."

I stared out across what was left of the marina; at the crystal clear water and the reddening sky—in which a solitary pterodactyl whirled—and the golden clouds, like heaps of fleece pillows. Her tone of voice had given me pause. "Sure. I—I was re-checking the Big Game. The Bar and Grill. I'll ... I'll head up right now."

And I went, hurrying to where the Jeep was parked in front of the Sue and Joy General Store and laying the flare gun on its passenger seat—before turning the ignition and heading up Bimini Bay Way, staring between houses as I drove and peering into their tall windows (although for what I wasn't sure; we'd already checked them for Búi and their original owners had long since vanished in the Flashback). It was easy to do; driving so carelessly—there weren't any other drivers or pedestrians to think about; only the Compies scattering before you like flightless gulls or the occasional newspaper or plastic bag. That's how it had been since the Event; and, as a consequence, you tended to get to where you were going quickly and effortlessly, before the melancholy of the place could really sink in (it was the seeing of it all at once that did it; the sheer totality of all that emptiness blurring past), something I was immensely grateful for as I turned left on Queen's Street and jounced onto the beach—and saw Amanda's Prius parked next to the overturned truck and custom boat trailer; next to which lay, well, whatever it was. Because it looked like a kind of miniature submarine, only shaped and painted like a shark, replete with rows of sharp teeth. It even had a dorsal fin.

"What the hell is it?" I asked, getting out, then hurried to help her as she shouldered her rifle and gripped the thing by a fin.

"Seriously?" she asked. The sand loosened and slid from its hull as we pulled the object upright. "It's a Seabreacher." She stood back and dusted her hands. "Sort of a jet ski, only enclosed. It—people use it to dive under the water ... then breach the surface, like a dolphin."

I stood and looked at it—at the Seabreacher. "Okay. Great. And this helps us—"

"Don't be obtuse." She moved forward and tried the hatch handle, which turned—then opened the cockpit, slowly. "Seats two. Might even be able to slip in a third. Knew a guy before the Flashback, said he could pilot his all the way to Miami. That's what I meant by, 'Don't be obtuse.' It means we're not stuck here."

I must have looked—unenthused.

"That's a good thing," she said. "In case you were wondering."

"A good thing," I said, and looked back the way I'd come.

"Yes, *a good thing.*"

I focused on the small church further back along the beach—Gateway Outreach Ministry—which we'd already checked. Except for the sacristy, which had been locked (this had been before we found the rifle). Wasn't it at least possible she'd taken refuge inside it?

"Sebastian ..."

The answer, of course, was no. She'd have responded when we called out (and we'd called out a *lot).* But what if she were sick, or wounded—unconscious, even? What if she'd been unable to hear us, or to respond even if she did? What if she'd been too debilitated to reach the door? Was it really magical thinking to suppose—

Amanda exhaled, defeated. "Sebastian ... what can I do?"

I turned to look at her as she shrunk down in the sand, looking more tired than any twentysomething had a right to—more haggard, her eyes vacant and puffy, her cheeks sallow. "I mean, how long do you think they'll last? One small, overgrown grocery store ... and a mini food-mart? (by 'overgrown' she'd meant the ubiquitous moss and vine—presumably prehistoric—which had come, along with the Compies and the pterodactyls, immediately after the Flashback) Six months? Couple of years—if we're lucky?"

I scanned the nearby homes. "Longer than that. Plus there's the bars and restaurants—not to mention all the houses." I looked at the darkening horizon. "It'll be light for a while. We should keep searching."

I felt her eyes follow me as I walked toward the Jeep.

"Sometimes I don't know what you want from me," she said.

I paused before climbing in. "I want you to help me find my wife," I said.

After which, realizing how cruel that had been, how unfair (for she'd been helping me tirelessly), I added, "You should get some rest. It's—it's going to be dark. I'll push on from here; okay? Don't wait up."

And I put the Jeep in gear.

The first thing I noticed when I got home to the duplex—it must have been around midnight—was that Amanda's unit was dark while mine was illuminated; something quickly explained when I swung open the door and saw the burning candles, not to mention the tinfoil-covered plate and half bottle of wine; or, for that matter, the greeting card-sized envelope—from which I withdrew a letter that read, simply, Happy 50th, S.B. *We'll find her.*

I guess I must have smiled.

"S.B." –*Sebastian Adams.* She had a memory like a steel trap.

I lifted the tinfoil and peeked at the dish—a fusilli pasta topped with white marinara sauce—but wasn't any hungrier than the last time she'd cooked; and merely re-covered it. I looked around the table. That wine, though.

I snatched it up and fetched a glass (funny she hadn't left me one) and then went out onto the deck—startling a Compy in the process, which leapt from the round table next to my chair and strutted—its little head bobbing, its tail jouncing—across the planks; into the cycad bushes.

"Boo," I said.

Then I settled in: propping my feet on the stool and looking out at the Atlantic, purposefully ignoring the little framed picture of Búi; disregarding the spilled peanuts and disturbed water glasses, some of which had been knocked over and some of which remained standing, but all of which contained or had contained small amounts of water, because now *I* was doing it (wasn't it funny, how couples could rub off on each other?).

"Tomorrow we'll do Resorts World," I said, still not looking at the picture. "If that's okay with you. I mean, it's like I've always said: You're the boss. No, no, that's how I want it. You should know that by now."

I took a drink straight from the bottle, which Amanda had left open, and exhaled. Then I tipped it again and drained the entire contents. "Well, honey, you wanted purple yams, remember? But it looks like your *dinky dau* sense of direction finally got the best of you. So you lost your way and mistook north for south; and now you're probably on the other side of Bailey Town–alone, confused, and terrified, I'm sure."

I looked at the sky–just a vast, black pit, mostly, like the ocean–but didn't see any lights, nor the prism-like jewels that had hung there since the Flashback–the time-storm; whatever–I suppose because of the clouds.

"Or ... have you disappeared to somewhere else; like everyone else on this island? Another time, another place, another epoch ..." I lolled my head against the backrest, woozily. "What the hell is this Flashback, anyway? I'll tell you what I think; I'm afraid Time itself has somehow been changed so that half the planet never existed. I'm afraid the first wave took the others and the second wave brought the dinosaurs and a third wave, well, a third wave took you. Because, honey, I've searched ... and searched ... and you just don't seem to be here. Not fucking anywhere."

A moment came and went; a moment in which I might have shattered, a moment in which I was capable of anything. But, as I said: It came ... and it went.

And then I *did* look at her picture; at her round, youthful face (although we were both precisely the same age), and her large, straight teeth. At the big brown eyes I'd often joked would eventually outgrow their sockets (to just dangle from their stalks, I'd said), and her ability to smile for the camera even after a terrifying ride in Miami (with a drunken boat captain) had almost ended our vacation—and our lives. At the girl from Bình Du'o'ng Province, South Vietnam, whom I'd married 7 years prior and experienced the initial Flashback with—as well as the meteor-caused tsunami which had happened immediately after—but who had then vanished without a trace on a trip to get purple yams. And chia seeds.

I laughed a little at that in the warm, bitter darkness, wondering if she'd ever found them.

"I bet you did," I said, my faculties beginning to fade, the wine beginning to kick my ass, before reaching out and laying the picture face-down on the table.

And then I slept, and eventually dreamed; of the island as seen from the heavens and of floating through a kind of limbo, a kind of purgatory. Of passing over Alice Town and Bailey Town and on to the open sea, which was infinite. Of being joined by another so close that our wings brushed, and flying—not like Icarus, not like Daedalus—but purposefully, fearlessly, without regret, into the ancient, seething, fire-pit cauldron of the sun.

Of what went through my mind when I saw the turkey-sized predators congregating at the end of the jetty (or rather the start, for we were heading back toward shore from the ferry terminal), I have no memory; other than to say I'd felt suddenly good, suddenly content, while striding along beside Amanda over the lapping surf (and laughing at some joke), and that, when I saw the predators, all of that just went away, just drained from the world, like the sun going behind a cloud.

Because it *had* been a good day; the first since Búi had disappeared. Nor could I put my finger on why, exactly: maybe it was simply because the weather had been so agreeable; or because the company had been so good. Maybe it was because we'd cleared an entire block of houses as well as the ferry by late afternoon and I'd been reminded of just how many places—safe places—she could still be. Or maybe it was because I'd forgotten, however briefly, that the world was a necropolis: a windswept graveyard, and that we—Amanda and I—were likely the last living souls.

Until we were coming back along the jetty from the ferry, that is. Until the slim, lithe predators with their long, dark tails and blue-gray coastal-patterns; their white, unblinking eyes, their little, undulating mohawks comprised of blood-red feathers, saw us.

"Are those—what did you call them? Comp—compsognathuses?" asked Amanda. "They don't look the same, for some reason."

I peered at the animals—just animals—through the shimmering heat: the three of them having become four, the four of them about to become five (as yet another emerged from behind an abandoned SUV) ... no, *six.*

"No," I said, absently. "I don't think so. They're too big."

I watched as the things seemed to focus on us, one of them shaking off while another used a foreclaw to scratch itself behind the ear. "Plus, they've got longer arms. And those toe claws; they're extendable–you can see it from here. More like a deinonychus (I had a dinosaur encyclopedia back at the duplex), or a–"

"Or a what?" She stared at the animals as though she were seeing a ghost. "Or a velociraptor, like in *Jurassic Park?"* She started to back up. "Because if that's what you were going to say, *don't.* Besides, they're too small."

"Movies exaggerate," I said–also backing up. "Just easy does it. They're as scared of us as we are of them."

But now there were more, about twelve at least (with still more streaming in), one of which darted forward abruptly ... and then hesitated, craning its neck to look at the others and shrieking–angrily, it seemed–just like a bird.

"Yeah," said Amanda. "That's bullshit. Look at them. There's strength in numbers."

Alas, I *was* looking at them, at their eerily intense focus (like cats starring at a pair of robins) and their coiled shanks; at their tails which were moving back and forth like knives.

I felt my vest for the other flares and touched the heel of my knife. "They're going to try and rush us; we're going to have to run for it. Are you up to it? I'm thinking all the way to the ferry ... how about it?"

"It'll bring them on, I guarantee it ..." She unslung her rifle and looked over her shoulder. "I don't think we can make it. I mean—wait ... what about that island shuttle?"

I watched as the others filed after the first and they regrouped—just a gaggle of heads and tails—then glanced at it myself. "Forget it. It's got a canvas roof—remember?"

"With steel ribs, though."

"Yeah, but—we'd be *stuck.* There's no key."

And then they were coming, not in a gaggle but in a staggered formation, bounding forward but in turns, running and pausing, as we turned and flat-out bolted—sprinting for the ferry as the sun shone hot and merciless and without compassion; veering for the island shuttle once we realized we'd never make it, piling through its driver's door and slamming it behind us as the raptors fell upon the vehicle like a threshing machine and began climbing and tearing at its canopy.

"Wait, don't—"

My ears rung as she started firing, blindly, into the animals, at least two of the slugs hitting the beams and ricocheting—one of them close enough to nick my ear.

"There's too many of them," I shouted, even as a dark snout stabbed between the beams and banged to a halt, gnashing its teeth. "Just stay low, they can't get through."

After which I eased the rifle from her hands and we hunkered near the floor; the raptors screaming and tearing the roof apart even as ragged pieces of it fell and they began reaching between its beams with their human-like forelimbs—swiping at us with their curved talons, blindly; reaching and groping and searching—like zombies.

Neither of us behaved bravely or kept our wits about ourselves. It was the screams that were the worst; which tore through the air like knives—like fighter jets passing so close you could see the rivets. Which split your mind so that you were too disoriented to think, to do much of anything. I'm afraid they got the better of us both as we cowered near the floor and covered our ears; as Amanda reached for me and pulled me close and I wrapped her up in my arms and squeezed her tight.

"Just hold me," she said, as the entire vehicle rocked and shook around us. "And don't let go."

And so I held her and didn't let go; cradling her head in my hands as the raptors screamed and continued their assault—as the entire truck was lifted on one side only to crash back down, as she said almost softly, "We—we have a responsibility. I never told you. A purpose. Because ... we're the last, and someone ... someone has to continue. Do you understand what I'm saying?"

I squeezed her tighter even as the glass and canvas rained down. *"Shhh,* save your strength. They'll give up and go away ... we just have to wait. Just—hang in there."

More broken glass; more shredded canvas. I squeezed my eyes shut; I was no longer certain they wouldn't get in.

"I want you to promise me, Sebastian. Promise me you'll meet me there—no matter what. Because if not us, then who?"

The raptors cried out in unison—like a perverse choir; it was almost as though they were celebrating, like this was their victory song.

I pulled back enough to look at her; at her dark blue eyes, so much like my own, and her youthful face—which was beautiful by any measure—understanding with perfect clarity what she'd meant; and realizing, too, to my great and utter astonishment, that I agreed; that we owed the world that, every bit as much as I owed Búi. That it was our duty, in a sense ... to ensure the bloodline survived; to propagate the species. And I realized something else, now that we were so close we could smell each other's sweat and I could feel the back of her hair against my hand and her body pressed against my own—like a rock; now that I had a raging hard-on in the face of what seemed certain death, God help me. And that was that I *wanted to live.*

Irregardless of if we found Búi or not; I wanted to live—to continue the journey—to spit in the eye of whatever had selected me for extinction, whatever had selected Búi for extinction, selected the *whole world.* Whatever had just crossed us out like a grammatical error: 'Remove this,' and scrubbed us from the sands of Time.

That's when we noticed it; at precisely the same instant, I'm sure. That the sound and the chaos had stopped. That the raptors, the screamers, the bloody *things,* had called off their attack. That the world had gone quiet again and we could hear the water lapping against the jetty's pilings.

We disengaged from each other and got up—looked out the driver's side window.

The majority of the horde was gone. We were still trapped; there remained about six animals—yes, six, exactly—but the larger pack, the larger pod, herd, murder, whatever, was gone.

I picked up the flare gun (which I'd found in the wreckage of a yacht after the tsunami, when Búi was still here), and unsheathed my knife. Amanda did the same, chambering a round in the Marlin rifle and taking out her own knife.

We never discussed it; never weighed the pros and cons of what we were about to do, never questioned what we were both feeling, which was that we wanted to live, and to not be afraid. We never asked the other if it was the right thing or the wrong thing—if it was worth the risk, say, when the other raptors could come screaming back at any moment. We already knew it was the right thing, because it was the only thing. Instead I just gripped the door handle and looked at her, and when she was ready—she nodded.

And then I threw open the door and we piled out.

There were six of them, as I said—all of whom rushed us the instant our feet touched the ground. All of whom snarled and charged us like wolverines as we raised our weapons and fired—the flare gun cracking and hissing, blanching the scarlet haze (for the sun had painted everything red and gold), its projectile punching through one of the raptors' chests and lighting it up so that its ribs were backlit briefly and I could see, if only for an instant, its burning, beating heart.

Yet still they came, another one leaping at me even as I dropped the gun—which clattered against the planks—as I dropped it and grabbed the thing by its neck—then brought the knife down with my other hand and stabbed it between the eyes.

"Run!" I shouted, even as Amanda shot another—her second—and then bolted toward the shore, drawing the others so that I was able to snatch up the flare gun and quickly reload it; so that I was able to pursue them and to shoot one in the back—while Amanda turned and took out the last of them (shooting it in the head so that the back of its skull exploded like a spaghetti dinner thrown against the wall; so that it collapsed, writhing, about 10 feet in front of her—whereupon she quickly approached it and shot it again, just to be sure).

And then she looked at me (as the dead and dying animals lay all around us) and I looked back: our chests heaving; our faces covered in sweat, our worn clothes bloody and disheveled, and I knew that *she* knew—which was that today *we* were the predators, the thing needing to be feared—the killers. And that neither of us needed to worry; not about food or other predators or mysterious lights in the sky or anything. Because we were the masters of our fate, we and no one else, not even God. And we were the master of the world's fate, too.

At which she ran to me and we collided and I held her fast, there on the long jetty in the Atlantic Ocean (in the Bermuda Triangle), there beneath a day moon and the blood-red sky, in an instant in which it was good, so very good, not to be afraid, not to be alone. And as to what may or may not have happened in those breaths, those pulse points between that moment and the next—the next day, the next search, the next milestone; as to that, I offer only a quote from Gandhi: "Speak only if it improves upon the silence."

It's possible I'd never felt so alive as when we took the Seabreacher out the next day. All I know for certain is that diving into the gurgling darkness at 50 miles per hour (and then breaching again, like a dolphin) turned out to be a lot of fun; so much so that we spent the better part of the morning doing just that: diving and breaching, plunging and rising, racing up and down the island (and around its horn, to Pigeon Cay) like damn fools; like college kids on a spring break, which I suppose Amanda was.

That is, until we broke surface and saw the meteor, which was arching across the sky like some orange and black torpedo—like some great, cyclopean flare—painting a trail of smoke and fire as though driven by God Himself; shedding chunks and pieces of itself, like an avalanche. Nor did we slow and try to see where it impacted but rather steered for the shore straight away, beaching the Seabreacher in the shallows near the Big Game Resort and Marina and popping its jetfighter-like hatch, clambering out of it swiftly as the meteor vanished beneath the eastern horizon and the sky exploded: first yellow, or rather a kind of golden amber, then orange, then pink, and finally, after several moments, blue again—although not before the shockwave hit us and blasted us off our feet—straight onto our backs.

"That ... that hit about the same distance away as the first one," I said—after we'd caught our breath and determined neither of us were seriously hurt. *"Holy shit."* I stood and dusted myself off, then peered at the glowing horizon. "Different location, but same basic distance." I must have looked white as a ghost. "Jesus—another P wave. Another primary. And that means—"

"Another *actual wave,"* said Amanda. "Another tsunami—headed this way."

She glared at me and I glared back, both of us knowing full well what that meant. We had about two hours. Two hours before it hit and all hell broke loose. At the max.

She looked at the Seabreacher, which gleamed in the sun, then into its cockpit. "We're going to need that fuel can; the one from the truck. And supplies: food, water, a way to start a fire—"

"Now wait just ... I can't—"

"Do you want to live or not?" she snapped—before placing her hands near the Seabreacher's caudal fin and pushing, trying to turn the boat around. "Because I do. And there's only a quarter tank left in this beast—which isn't enough."

I knelt beside her and helped; shoving as hard as I could, sinking and sliding in the sand—until we'd succeeded in turning the thing around.

"Okay," I said, leaning on the metal, our faces close. "I'll go to the duplex and get the gas—if you want to hit Sue and Joy's and see what you can find. Definitely some bottled water. And a lighter—several of them, if you can. Some toilet paper wouldn't hurt. We'll meet back here in, say—twenty minutes. No later. Okay?"

She looked at me uncertainly, compassionately. "You want to get your picture—don't you? I saw it next your chair. When I—when I left your birthday dinner."

I stared at her for a moment before lowering my gaze, focusing on the sand. "To prove she existed," I said, almost whispering. "To show that—that she was here. She deserves that." I looked out over the ocean. "So do I."

"Well—*go get it, then,* Sebastian. Go get it and get the gas can and get your ass back here. Because I can't do this alone."

And we went—on foot (our vehicles were still parked where we'd found the Seabreacher; on the opposite side of the island): Amanda splitting off for the General Store while I continued on to our duplex, which wasn't far. The hardened twentysomething going one way while I went another–haunted, guilt-ridden, alone.

Understand this: while it certainly *was* a T. rex–or something very much like it–it was not, by any stretch, a monster. It was not, for example, Godzilla (or any other behemoth as depicted in popular movies and books; including, I dare say, *Jurassic Park*). No, this was just an animal, big as an elephant, it's true (but no bigger), and yet, ultimately, no more outlandish than a spotted leopard or a crocodile (at least not since the Flashback); meaning it played well enough with its environment that I hadn't even noticed it–until it was too late.

Too late to get a shot in, anyway–not too late to run; which I did, dropping the gas can and bolting (even as the rex paused to sniff some spoor) before coming to a massive tree (a Caribbean pine, as I recall) and–after jamming the flare gun into my waistband–starting to scale it.

Alas, I'd barely attained the middle limbs when the T. rex arrived–its jaws snapping shut only inches from my shoes and its bellows echoing, furiously. Yet there was little it could do; I'd already climbed beyond its reach (and was climbing higher still). And so we tried to wait each other out, the tyrannosaur and I, as fragments of the meteor began lancing the earth and the doomsday tsunami drew inexorably closer. As the clock ticked mercilessly and Amanda surely fretted and Búi seemed almost to whisper in my ear: *Where have you gone to, my husband, my love, and why have you abandoned me? Is it not obvious–so very, very obvious—where I am? Why, oh why, can't you see?*

At which, inexplicably, I *did* see–something.

A roof.

Just a roof.

Indeed, there wasn't even anything special about it–this roof, other than it was attached to a house I had not seen from the ground–and so had not searched.

I rubbed my eyes and looked at it a second time.

How could we have missed that? Right here, in a wooded section of Alice Town? Right here–not even a block from the Big Game Club Resort and Marina?

I gazed out over the treetops, toward the ocean–and saw it. Saw the wave. Or at least a band of white along the horizon that *looked* like a wave. Was it possible? Búi–I mean? Had she gotten lost–or even injured–and just wandered into the first house she'd come to?

And did I have the time to find out?

And then something just snapped and I was taking out the flare gun and aiming it into the rex's mouth and squeezing the trigger—even as Amanda appeared at the corner of my vision and trained her rifle—after which the rex's maw lit up like a firework and blood jetted from its head (for that's where Amanda had shot it) and the tyrant lizard just collapsed—not threshing about like in the movies, not unfurling its foam latex or CGI tail, but simply slumping forward into the grass like a beached whale until the tip of its snout touched the tree and it was gone. After which I quickly climbed down.

"See?" she said, and chambered a new round. "We make a helluva team." She frowned a little as though she'd just thought of something. "Where's the gas?"

I nodded to where I'd dropped it—about 50 feet away.

"Thank God," she said. She slung the rifle over her shoulder and moved toward it—then paused. "What's wrong?"

I think I just stared at the ground. "I—I spotted something ... up there in the tree. Something we missed. It ... it's in that woodland—right next to the duplex." I lifted my eyes to look at her. "An entire house."

She only gazed at me, saying nothing.

"So, what," she said, finally, "You're just going to mosey back up there and check it out—with the wave practically on top of us? Is that it?"

I nodded, slowly. "Yeah. That's about it." I reached out to touch her but she slapped my hand away. "I'm sorry," I said.

She glared at me as though she might strike me. "Oh, you will be, Sebastian. You will be. Just as soon as that wave arrives." She started to storm off but stopped on a dime. "And for what? Another empty house? Another room full of ghosts? Because there is *nothing here,* Sebastian. *We're it."* Again she started to go, and again she stopped. "What–you think you're the only one who's lost someone? The only one who's lost a wife, or a child, or their parents? Well, I've lost people too–everyone I've ever known. I did! Amanda Everett." Her eyes welled up suddenly and profusely and she swiped at them. "Just because I'm younger than you doesn't make it any easier. And yet we've been given this *chance,* Sebastian. This one chance to face it together; to reboot the world. To literally save it. *To make babies,* for God's sake. And you just want to—you want to—"

And she came at me and we collided, briefly, before embracing–not forcibly (even violently), as had been the case on the jetty, but gently, softly. And then I handed her the flare gun.

"Take it–please," I said. "It–it needs to be with you. And the boat."

She hesitated, staring at the thing, before offering me the rifle, which I declined. Then she took it—the flare gun—decisively, resolutely, and stuffed it beneath her waistband.

"I'm going to wait for you as long as I possibly can, okay? Understand? Five minutes before I leave—I'm gonna to shoot a flare; that'll be your signal to drop anything you're doing and to run, not walk, back to this location." She stared at me with conviction. "Okay?"

"Look, you don't have to—"

"Ah, but I do," she said, and held out her palm. "No less than you have to go check out that house. The flares, please."

I dug them out of my jacket and handed them to her—there were only three. "You shouldn't wait too long. I mean, who knows how big this one will be, or how fast it's moving. But okay. One flare equals five minutes." I stepped back to look at her—to take all of her in. "It—it wasn't just because—"

"Shuttup. Just ... just go do what you got to do. All right?"

She moved to leave but paused.

"Five minutes," she repeated, and then really did go.

What was I feeling as I ascended the stairs to the upper (and last) bedroom of the house? It's impossible to describe; other than to say 'despair' is too weak an expression. No, this was hopelessness and anguish as I could not have imagined—not in my loneliest dreams and nightmares—made worse, no doubt, by my fantasizing along the way; by my sheer, undiluted optimism that each step had somehow brought me closer to my Omega Point, closer to Búi.

But the steps had not been kind—nor had they been quick. And by the time I opened that final door to the final room I had largely succumbed to the inevitable; by which I mean I hardly gave the space a glance—seeing only a jumble of blankets on a four-poster bed and a rickety nightstand crowded with half-emptied bottles of water—before quickly turning to leave.

At which, before I'd even gained the stairs, I froze. Dead in my tracks.

The bottles of water. The plastic containers labelled Aquafina and Dasani—all of them half-full.

My heart thumped against my chest.

"Honey?" I said, in the near perfect silence, "Are you there?"

And then I waited; feeling that even an apparition; even a ghost, a chimera, would be welcome. But there was nothing. Not so much as a creak in the floor. Not so much as a rustling curtain.

But then there *was* something. Just the smallest of voices—indeed, a sound so faint I might have imagined it. Just a small, feint voice which said, simply: "Honey? Is that you?"

And—*Dear God*—I scrambled; rushing back into the room without a moment's hesitation; finding her head exposed outside the tangle of pillows and blankets.

"Honey! Honey!" I knelt beside her at the head of the bed—between her and the open, curtainless window—placing my hands upon her: one on her stomach and one on her head. "Are you all right? Jesus, how have you ..." I looked around the room and saw several empty cans—Dinty Moore Stew and Jack Mackerel, mostly, one of which was entertaining a rat. "Can you move? Can you move, honey? 'Cuz we gotta get you out of here. And I mean, like, *now.*"

I suppose that's when I noticed it; that her eyes were jaundiced and her skin had turned a sickly yellow. And I knew, also, even before I asked her (and she explained it), precisely what had happened: for she had been bitten by something poisonous—a breed of Compy, she said—and had stumbled her way into the house, where she'd been lying, delirious and partially paralyzed, for some three and a half weeks now. Nor was she going anywhere, because the paralysis had presented itself as a kind of full-body muscle spasm, which meant even the slightest movement could cause her excruciating pain.

"But where—where are we now?" she managed—and was interrupted by a coughing jag. "I mean, I remember getting lost; and I remember being bitten, and I remember being stuck in a house for a long, long time. But what I don't remember is how I got *here* ... with you."

I moved to respond but paused, listening. For there was a sound now. A kind of low rumble—which rattled the panes.

I clasped her hand in mine and stroked her forehead, tidied the strands of hair. "We're home, honey. We're back home now. In our stupid little apartment. And—well, it's been a wonderful day, just really nice. We went to Greenbluff—do you remember? To pick cherries. And you picked so many you could hardly carry your buckets, so I had to do it for you—as well as carry my own; but that was all right because I started singing "Beast of Burden" by the Rolling Stones—you know, how I do: badly—and it made you laugh; which to me has always been the best sound in the world. And then we went and got pizza and ate it in the car, and after that, went to my Dad's—to celebrate his 89th birthday. And it was wonderful, just wonderful, with all of us there and the dogs chewing on our shoes and the sky sheltering everything like a big, blue dome; and later, like a dark umbrella."

I heard a *crack!* and a *whoosh* and a *fizzle* and looked out the window; saw the flare rising high like a rocket bound for the Moon: just rising and rising and levelling off–even hovering, briefly, like a UFO–before beginning its glorious fall, its sparkling and brilliant demise, its deep and fatal dive into the Big, Vast Nothing.

She rolled her head on the large, dirty pillow. "Is it–is it the Fourth of July? Are we watching fireworks?"

"Yes, sweetheart, we are." I moved out of her line of sight. *"Look at it, sweetie.* See how it sparks and shines."

"It's so beautiful," she said. "But what–what on earth is that other thing? That sound? It's like–it's like thunder, almost. Or an earthquake."

I moved around to the other side of the bed and got in–nuzzling up against her, holding her so we were perfect spoons. "It's the fireworks, honey, echoing off the buildings. It's nothing to be afraid of. Just a sound. Remember–remember when we went to the Air Show that year, and the sound of the jets scared you so bad that you started hyperventilating? And do you remember what I said to you, that you should just count to 10–and breathe?"

She nodded, her black hair tickling my nose, as the rumbling became a thunder, and then a *roar.*

"Try that now, okay, sweetie? Just count to ten and breathe, all right? Go ahead."

And she started counting, her voice clear and child-like, her accent as strong as ever. "One (inhalation) ... two (inhalation) ... three ... four ..."

"Remember to breathe, honey; do it after every number. I'm right here. *We're all here.* Your children and your parents and my Dad and all your friends. We're in this together—every one of us. And I love you. More than you will ever know. Goodnight, honey."

"Eight ... nine ... ten." There was a moment of silence, or so it seemed. "I love you too, sweetheart."

And then came the waters, surging, crashing, churning, roaring.

And we just breathed.

Deeply.

And yet we did not die—not really. Rather, it felt as though I slept, dreaming ... of the island as seen from the heavens and of floating through a kind of limbo, a kind of purgatory. Of passing over Alice Town and Bailey Town and finally out to sea: where a grain of rice turned out to be the Seabreacher. Of watching that Seabreacher skip and jounce over (and through) the waves like a dolphin–heading toward Miami–and knowing, somehow (for I could see the future now as though it were laid out before me, like a tapestry), that it contained not just Amanda but the dreams and aspirations of all mankind; and that I'd had a part in that.

And, lastly, of being joined by another–so close that our wings brushed–and flying, not like Icarus, not like Daedalus, but purposefully, fearlessly, without regret, into the ancient, seething, fire-pit cauldron of the sun.

If you enjoyed this work of fiction, please consider leaving a review at your point of sale. Thanks!

www.ingramcontent.com/pod-product-compliance
Lightning Source LLC
LaVergne TN
LVHW012056160826
845678LV00014B/2843

* 9 7 9 8 7 2 8 6 3 2 5 5 9 *